MARK BATTERSON
AND JOEL N. CLARK

JACK STAPLES AND THE POET'S STORM

DAVID C COOK

transforming lives together

JACK STAPLES AND THE POET'S STORM
Published by David C Cook
4050 Lee Vance Drive
Colorado Springs, CO 80918 U.S.A.

Integrity Music Limited, a Division of David C Cook
Eastbourne, East Sussex BN23 6NT, England

The graphic circle C logo is a registered trademark of David C Cook.

This story is a work of fiction. All characters and events are the product of the author's
imagination. Any resemblance to any person, living or dead, is coincidental.

LCCN 2014957984
ISBN 978-0-8307-7597-2
eISBN 978-0-8307-7650-4

© 2015, 2018 Mark Batterson, Joel N. Clark
Published in association with the literary agency of The Fedd
Agency, Inc., Post Office Box 341973, Austin, Texas 78734.

The Team: Alex Field, Jamie Chavez, Nick Lee,
Jennifer Lonas, Helen Macdonald, Karen Athen
Cover Design and Photos: Kirk DouPonce, DogEared Design; iStock

Printed in the United States of America

First Edition 2015

3 4 5 6 7 8 9 10

062918

Juno Jehan and Elah Mandela, you
are the true Heroes of the Ages. Now
and forever, you have my heart.

Chapter 1

THE POET'S COFFER

The wonder of riding a flying fox had faded long ago. Two days crouched on its back with little sleep or chance to stretch her legs had left Alexia Dreager tired and sore. She'd named the fox Dagger because of the way it flew. Dagger had the precision of an eagle and the agility of a sparrow, changing direction and darting here and there without warning.

Alexia hugged Dagger close as he dove straight down, then turned sharply to the left. Her fists tightened on handfuls of fur as the fox soared toward the face of an enormous bluff, then twisted sideways and entered a hidden cavern. The fox flipped upright as he glided inside, then dropped and skidded to a stop, sending dust and shale flying.

Alexia exhaled heavily before climbing from his back. Every muscle burned, and she was weary beyond words, yet she took the time to scratch Dagger behind the ears. *"You did well,"* she sent the thought as Dagger yawned widely. She cleared her mind and waited, but nothing came; the poor beast collapsed in exhaustion.

In the past two days Alexia had spent much of her time trying to communicate with Dagger. It was the strangest thing she'd ever done, and she still wasn't sure it was actually happening. More than once an image had formed unbidden in her mind, and she was certain it had come from Dagger. *I just need to learn how to understand what the images mean,* she thought. *And to figure out how to make him understand me!*

Alexia turned to watch as more flying beasts entered the cavern, each landing with varying degrees of grace. First was a winged black panther carrying a bleary-eyed Jack Staples. Next came Wild on an overly large meerkat, followed by Arthur Greaves, who still slept on the back of a winged beaver. Alexia could barely believe it; the boy had slept through most of the past two days, waking only to eat or relieve himself.

The giant, Andreal, was on a very large and very beleaguered winged rabbit. Every time Alexia saw Andreal climb onto the hare's back, the poor animal let out an audible sigh before launching into the air. Mrs. Dumphry was last; her tusked elephant had two sets of wings that scraped the sides of the cavern. The ancient woman hadn't been the same these past two days. Aias, the man she'd loved for more then five thousand years, had died in the City of Shadows.

Alexia's friends climbed down and stretched tired muscles as the rest of the Clear Eyes collapsed in exhaustion. Clear Eyes was the Awakened's name for animals that had chosen to serve the Author.

"I do not understand," Andreal rumbled. He stretched his arms high, his fingers brushing the cavern ceiling. "We should be losing them ages ago. How be it they still be finding us?" He sat heavily on the cavern floor. Andreal reminded Alexia of a bear she'd once known back at the circus.

"A tired body can betray even the most willing mind," Mrs. Dumphry said as she rubbed her eyes. "I do not know how they continue to follow, yet I am sure the answer is simple. I am just too weary to see it."

Some version of this conversation came up each time they'd stopped over the past two days. Ten thousand of the Assassin's deadliest warriors had been pursuing them ever since they'd escaped the City of Shadows. At first Mrs. Dumphry hadn't been worried. She was sure the Clear Eyes could fly faster than the Shadow Souled's winged beasts; yet no matter how fast they'd gone, they'd been unable to stay more than a few hours ahead of the dark army.

Alexia was as vexed as the others, but for different reasons. On the day they escaped the Assassin's city, she'd learned something so incredible, she could still barely believe it. Her mother might still be alive. Until then, she'd been sure her mother had passed away when Alexia was just five years old. She had no way of knowing for certain, but it was possible that Madeleine Dreager was out there somewhere.

Yet it wasn't just hope for her mother that occupied Alexia's thoughts. Each hour spent fleeing the dark army took them farther away from the City of Shadows. With each passing hour, Alexia's guilt and misery grew. Though she and a few of her friends had been rescued,

Alexia's best friends, her Gang of Rogues, had been left behind. *It's the second time I've abandoned them.* She shivered at the thought.

Each hour also took her farther from her friends, who were most likely being tortured and starved. *If they're still alive,* she thought. She had no way of knowing who had survived the battle or whether the Assassin would bother keeping any of the prisoners alive. The Last Battle had begun; what need did he have of prisoners? Alexia didn't care about being one of the Children of Prophecy or about what the Awakened expected of her. The only things that mattered were finding her mother and saving her friends.

She hadn't told anyone what she'd learned about her mother, in part because there had been little time to talk since their escape, and in part because she was afraid to. Although she no longer hated Mrs. Dumphry, Alexia still didn't know what to think of her. But she was certain Mrs. Dumphry would never allow her to run off. *I am one of the Children of Prophecy, after all,* she thought glumly. Besides, Alexia had no idea where to look for her mother or how to save her friends, and the only person she could think to ask was Mrs. Dumphry.

Even if I knew where Mother was or could sneak back to the City of Shadows, could I do any of it by myself? She'd spent many years on her own but had been in a different world from the one she was in now. The Last Battle had begun, and Mrs. Dumphry said that all of creation was making its choice—the Author or the Assassin. From Dagger's back, Alexia had seen things she still didn't understand. The trees of an entire forest had thrashed about as if fighting one another. Later she'd seen a lake turn black as pitch within seconds, the smell of death rising high into the air. Alexia had counted five earthquakes in the past two days, and Dagger had needed to fly around a number of tornadoes and one hurricane.

Something was wrong with the weather. It was as if the natural progression of things had been interrupted. Winter should lead to spring, spring to summer, and summer to fall. It was this rhythm that allowed the land to bear fruit and the soil to grow rich. Yet over the past two days, it was as if the weather had forgotten its place. There was no rhyme or reason for what happened between one hour and the next. The small band of Awakened had flown through a blizzard straight into a heat wave.

"Where are we?" a voice said from behind her.

Alexia turned to see Arthur Greaves awake. "You look horrible!" Arthur gasped as he met Alexia's eyes. "You should really get some sleep or something. I feel great! I've had the craziest dreams you can imagine. We were all riding on the backs of flying—" Arthur stopped as his eyes landed on the beaver. "Wait. What?" He squinted at the other beasts, then grinned. "That's amazing! Is that how we escaped the City of Shadows? The last thing I remember is seeing Andreal and Mrs. Dumphry fighting in the corridors of the coliseum. And where is Elion? Is she here too, or was that just a dream? She was flying beside me for a time. And what happened to the rest of the prisoners? Did everyone get out? I can't believe animals can fly! Jack, did you ever imagine such a thing?"

"Arthur Greaves," Mrs. Dumphry said, "it's time you learn to tame your tongue. An untamed tongue is far more dangerous than an untrained sword." She sighed as Arthur blushed, then walked over and placed a hand on his shoulder. "It is good to see you awake, child. You've been sleeping for two days, and much has happened. I am sure your friends will catch you up, but right now I need silence if I am to think."

Arthur's jaw dropped. "Two days," he mouthed as Jack wrapped an arm around him and walked Arthur toward the back of the cavern, quietly explaining what Arthur had missed. Arthur squealed at something Jack said, and Alexia smiled. She'd once thought the boy to be a coward, but she'd been wrong. He did have that habit of squealing like a little girl, and his stomach was weaker than most, but he was no coward. Arthur Greaves had single-handedly saved every one of them in the City of Shadows. Her memory was clear.

Alexia and the others had been buried beneath a mountain of a hundred thousand Shadow Souled. Then in walked Arthur Greaves. *No,* Alexia remembered, *in danced Arthur Greaves.* Liquid light flowed around him, forming a wall that plowed through the mountain of dark flesh. Without Arthur, none of them would have lived long enough for Elion to rescue them.

Alexia unfurled her blanket, then grabbed some bread and cheese from a sack she'd tied to Dagger's back. She bit off a chunk of cheese and sat down on the cold stone. Wild walked over to sit beside her.

"Where do you think we are?" Alexia asked.

"I heard Mrs. Dumphry say something about Morocco," Wild said through a yawn, "though I don't know for sure." His hair was tight ringlets, and his eyes had an orange tinge to them.

His name suits him, she thought.

She broke off a hunk of cheese and handed it to him. "We can't keep going like this," she said. "Surely the Shadow Souled must be as tired as we are. How do they keep finding us?"

"I don't know." Wild rubbed at his eyes. "But I'm sure Mrs. Dumphry will figure it out before long."

Mrs. Dumphry stood at the entrance to the cavern, staring out at the noonday sky.

"I saw her when I was with the Assassin," Alexia said without thinking. "He showed me a memory that was more than five thousand years old, and Mrs. Dumphry was there. And so was Aias."

Wild turned to stare at Alexia with awe-filled eyes. "So you saw her stab the poet? And you saw him rise from the dead a few minutes later?"

"I ... well, no." Alexia hadn't thought anyone knew the truth about Mrs. Dumphry. "No, the Assassin took me out of the memory just after she stabbed the poet. I didn't see what happened next." Alexia thought for a moment. "Does everyone know about her and Aias?"

Wild's expression became grim. The loss of Aias was hitting everyone hard. He had been the father of the Awakened just as Mrs. Dumphry was their mother. "I don't know what Mrs. Dumphry is going to do without him," Wild said.

Alexia nodded. She could picture Aias battling in the shadowed city. He danced among hundreds of Shadow Souled, his sword a blur of death. And still they couldn't touch him. She hadn't seen the moment of his death. But she'd seen him lying in the middle of the street with a spear in his chest. Within seconds the dark servants had swarmed over him.

"So that's why you trusted him." There was no accusation in Wild's voice, just a simple statement. "That's why you almost joined the Assassin. You thought Mrs. Dumphry killed the poet and then lied about it."

"That's part of it," she said. "But I also thought Korah was my father."

Wild's eyebrows rose, but he didn't question her. Korah was Alexia's uncle—her father's twin. Alexia had been told her uncle had died years before she was born, but that obviously hadn't been true. Her uncle had pretended to be her father, and to Alexia's great shame, she had believed him. On the day of their escape from the City of Shadows, she'd used a Memory Stone to go back and see the truth. Korah had killed her father and had tried to kill her mother.

"Mrs. Dumphry and Aias were the first humans to ever awaken," Wild said. "The story is legend among the Awakened. The poet himself, the Author made flesh, touched her eyes and removed the scales. He forgave her for what she'd done and saved her and Aias from the Assassin. The poet took them somewhere far away and stayed with them only a few minutes, but in that time, he asked for their help. They were to prepare the world for the Last Battle. They were to gather the Awakened and seek out the Chosen One, who would give birth to the Child of Prophecy."

Alexia didn't know what to say. She'd disliked Mrs. Dumphry from the moment they met. She'd refused to listen, fought her at every turn, and acted like a child. Now Alexia watched as Mrs. Dumphry stood with her arm outstretched, as if feeling the air. It was hard to believe she'd spent the better part of five thousand years searching for Alexia and Jack.

"Wait, what do you mean the poet rose from the dead?"

Wild grinned. "I wasn't sure you heard me. The Assassin demanded that Mrs. Dumphry bow before him and serve him forever. But she refused. And just as he was about to kill her, the poet rose from the dead and saved her."

Although Alexia was mesmerized by Wild's story, she couldn't stop thinking about his hands. They were holding hers as he talked, though he didn't seem to notice.

"It was the poet's death and resurrection that changed everything."

"What do you mean?" Alexia asked.

"That was the day the scales were weakened. And they've been falling from the eyes of humans ever since."

Alexia felt a fresh wave of guilt. She'd allowed the Assassin to manipulate her. She'd almost turned her back on her friends for the worst of reasons—power and fame.

"You can't beat yourself up about it." Wild seemed to understand what she was feeling. "He's called the Father of Lies for a reason."

"Would you have believed him?" Alexia made herself meet Wild's eyes.

"I might have. I don't think anyone knows how strong they are until they've been put to the test. In the end you did the right thing," he said. "It's not what we almost do that matters, only what we do. And in the face of sure death, you made the impossible choice."

He has beautiful eyes. Alexia blushed the moment the thought formed. For some reason, Wild did too, as he whipped his hands away.

"Is that why Mrs. Dumphry and Aias lived for so long?" Alexia cleared her throat, trying to act normal. "Because the poet gave them special powers?"

"No." Wild shook his head. "It was because they touched the poet's blood. Mrs. Dumphry says the blood of the poet is more powerful than we can imagine. Until two days ago, I didn't think anything could kill them."

"But how come Mrs. Dumphry looks so old, and Aias never seemed to age?"

Wild smiled. "Back then, Mrs. Dumphry wasn't just the queen of the world; she says she was also the most vain human to have ever lived. So when the poet told her and Aias they would live for thousands of years, he also told Mrs. Dumphry that she would continue to age so she would never have to struggle with vanity again!"

Alexia nodded. Through the Memory Stone, she'd seen the hundreds of mirrors that had surrounded Mrs. Dumphry's throne. Mrs. Dumphry had barely been able to tear her eyes from the mirrors even as she spoke to the poet.

"What is that?" Mrs. Dumphry's voice was a lightning crack. Alexia turned to see her staring at Arthur. "Arthur Greaves! What are you holding?" Mrs. Dumphry strode across the cavern to stand before Arthur and Jack. For a long moment, she stared at the small wooden box in Arthur's hands, her mouth agape.

Alexia had never imagined a day when Mrs. Dumphry would be speechless.

"Where … How did … Where did you get that?"

Andreal stepped closer as the others gathered to get a better look. "Do that be what I think it be?"

Alexia recognized the box in Arthur's hands. When she was living in the City of Shadows, she'd seen the Assassin holding it many times. Each time he noticed her watching, he'd wrapped it in shadows and hidden it away somewhere. The Assassin had seemed to both covet and fear the box.

"I stole it," Arthur said in a cautious tone. "It was after you and Aias and Andreal were taken." A pained look swept him. "I'm sorry. I just heard about Aias. I can't imagine how hard that must be."

Mrs. Dumphry wiped away a tear. "Please, finish your story."

"I was looking for somewhere to hide for the night because I didn't know what to do." He raised his hands defensively. "I know you all wanted me to go find Alexia and rescue her, but I didn't even know where to start. So I snuck into the big building or palace or whatever, and then the Shadowfog came. At least I think it was the Shadowfog from what Jack's told me about it."

Arthur began pacing as his voice rose. "I ran up the stairs—it sure was a lot of stairs by the way. There must have been, like, a hundred floors or something. And I think I found the Assassin's throne room, because there was a really big throne in it. That's when I saw this box hanging above it. The box was wrapped in shadows, but I felt it calling to me." Arthur turned to Jack. "Don't laugh, but I think it wanted me to come get it."

Alexia didn't think Jack was going to laugh. His eyes were glued to the box as if he, too, had seen it before.

"The thing is, when I tried to grab it, the shadows that were wrapped around it, or whatever, burned my hand something awful." He raised his hand to show Mrs. Dumphry the marks. "So I was going to leave, but then my name appeared on the box. It's not on it now, but it was! I'm not lying. It said, *Arthur Greaves: Loyal, Courageous, Warrior.*" Arthur flushed. "I'm not making it up; it's what the box said. And I know it's probably not true, but it was right here on the side." Arthur traced his finger along the side of the box as if offering proof. "And suddenly I felt like I couldn't leave without it. I know it was stealing, but I figured it was all right to steal from the Assassin. So anyway, that's when I started to dance"—Arthur blushed again—"and for some reason that worked."

Arthur seemed to search Mrs. Dumphry's face for some sign of what she was thinking. The longer Mrs. Dumphry stayed silent, the paler he became.

Mrs. Dumphry's hands shook as she reached for the box. Arthur handed it to her, and for a long moment, she cradled it as if it were the most important thing in the world. "Arthur Greaves"—her voice quivered—"you have no idea what you have done."

"I'm sorry!" Arthur wrung his hands. "I really didn't know. I never would have—"

"No. You have done something that should not have been possible. You have recovered the Poet's Coffer! We had no idea where it was or how to find it, but if the Awakened are to have any chance of surviving the Last Battle, we need it." Mrs. Dumphry glanced toward the cavern entrance. "I'm sure it is the reason the Shadow Army has been able to track us. To their eyes, this coffer would shine like a beacon in the night. They can feel its presence."

"I would have told you if I'd known. I would have—"

Mrs. Dumphry stepped forward and cupped Arthur's chin. "You saved us all from sure death at the Assassin's hand. And now you have done this. Arthur Greaves, I am honored to know you." She leaned in and kissed Arthur on the cheek. He blushed so furiously, Alexia wished she had an apple handy to compare which was redder.

"What is the Poet's Coffer?" Jack's eyes were glued to the box.

"The Assassin stole it from the poet after he died. I have been searching for it for as long as I searched for you and Alexia," Mrs. Dumphry said.

Alexia studied the box. There was nothing fancy about it. If she'd seen it in a shop, she wouldn't have looked twice.

"In the old days, poets made a living traveling between cities and towns. They told stories and juggled and did acrobatics. They played music and sang songs, and when they arrived in a town or village, crowds gathered to hear their stories and watch them perform." Mrs. Dumphry had a faraway look in her eyes. "In those days I didn't understand their importance. Now I know a good storyteller is far more powerful than any king or queen. All poets carried a coffer with them. It was where they kept their most prized possessions."

"What's inside? What was the poet carrying?" Arthur asked.

"I have no idea."

"So why do we need it?" Alexia asked. "Why is it so important in the Last Battle?"

"Because the poet told me it was." A smile crept along the corners of Mrs. Dumphry's lips. "Besides that, the same prophecy that speaks of you and Jack also mentions the coffer." Her voice took on a cadence as she recited, "'When the Awakened are destroyed and the foundations of the world have crumbled, from beneath the Assassin's Shadow the Child of Prophecy shall open the coffer to release the Poet's Storm.'"

Mrs. Dumphry shook her head. "Not even the Sephari know what it means, but it is clear at least one of the Children of Prophecy will need to open the coffer. Arthur Greaves, the fact that you took the coffer is as big a blow to the Assassin as losing the Children of Prophecy, perhaps bigger."

Alexia snickered. She'd been wrong. It was possible for Arthur to turn an even darker shade of red.

"Mrs. Dumphry"—Jack pulled a small leather fold from his cloak—"I think this might help you open it." He handed her the fold. "King Edward gave it to me when we were in Buckingham Palace. His family kept it safe for thousands of years so he could give it to me. I think it will help you open the coffer."

"Wait. What?" Arthur interrupted. "You met the king and didn't tell me? Did he have a crown? How can you be sure it was really him, and why would he give you an old pen anyway?"

Mrs. Dumphry sighed as the coffer disappeared up her sleeve. "Arthur Greaves," she said, studying the ancient quill, "wisdom and brevity are siblings. And while you have become friends with one, you have spurned the other."

A look of confusion crossed Arthur's face. He opened his mouth, then promptly closed it again.

"Jack, I would very much like to hear the story behind that pen. But I will not take it from you. If Edward's family kept it safe so he could give it to you, then you should keep it."

"But don't you want to open the coffer?"

"No, I do not. According to the prophecy, either you or Alexia need to open it. And though it did not specify whether it could be opened more than once, we do know it must be opened after the Awakened have been destroyed and the world has crumbled."

"I still don't understand," Alexia said. "Why did you search for so long to find me and Jack when the prophecy says we will destroy the world?"

"Because it also says you will save the world and defeat the Assassin," Mrs. Dumphry said cheerily.

"Mrs. Dumphry," Jack said. "I think I remember what we're meant to do next. At least I think I'm having the memory right now."

"You will have to talk once we're on our way," a voice called from the ledge of the cavern. It was Elion, a Sephari. Elion's skin sparkled like diamonds, the tops of her ears were pointed, and her eye color shifted according to her mood. She was from the world of Siyyon, home of the Author and birthplace of the Assassin. Elion could fly on her own and had circled back to get a better look at the Shadow Army. "The Shadow Souled will be here soon, and I am sorry to say we must flee yet again."

"That be impossible," Andreal rumbled. "They could no be coming so quickly."

"Only a fool questions what is, Andreal. And you are no fool," Mrs. Dumphry said.

"They are even wearier than we." Elion's eyes gathered the sunlight even as they shifted from crimson to stony gray. "But it is not just their desire to capture Jack and Alexia that has pushed them so hard." Elion cast Mrs. Dumphry a grim look. "An Odius leads them."

Andreal groaned, and Wild looked fearfully at Alexia.

"What's an Odius?" she whispered.

"It's death," he whispered back.

"The puzzle has come together." Mrs. Dumphry clapped her hands. "The dark army will be as afraid of the Odius as they are desperate to retrieve the Children of Prophecy and the coffer. With an Odius to lead them, they'll not give up until they've captured us or died from exhaustion. Young Jack and I will discuss his plan as we fly. But we leave now. In another twenty hours or so, we should come to an Oasis. The Author willing, we will have found a way to escape by then."

"Though you are correct that we must leave," Elion said, "let us wait a moment longer. I'm afraid I bring even worse news than that of the Odius." She turned to look out of the cavern. "The Assassin's Shadow comes. Even now it smothers the world with its embrace. I came as fast as I could so we could all stand beneath the sun together one last time. Come and drink in its light. Feel its warmth in your bones." Elion met Alexia's eyes as she approached the cavern mouth. "It may be the last time any of us see it again on this side of life."

Alexia had no idea what the Assassin's Shadow was, but she did as she was told. The sun shone bright, and not a cloud could be seen in the noonday sky. Elion gripped Alexia's hand and closed her eyes, turning her face to the sun.

Alexia was about to ask what was happening, when she saw it. A vast, slithering darkness was sweeping the land. It came from the south and spanned the horizon. Dread rose in her chest as her eyes lingered on the darkness.

"Do not waste a second watching this evil." Elion squeezed Alexia's hand warmly. "Turn your face to the sun and remember this moment."

The Awakened stood in silence as the darkness rocketed over them, swallowing the sky.

Chapter 2

A MEMORY OF
THINGS TO COME

The Assassin's Shadow radiated despair. Jack Staples could feel its touch on his skin. Whereas the sun brought life and warmth, the Assassin's Shadow brought only misery. From the back of his winged panther, Jack pulled his cloak closed. *The sun is gone, and we may never see it again!* It was a chilling thought.

He glanced upward, shielding his eyes against the slithering darkness. *How do we fight the sky?* It hadn't even been a full day since the darkness had come, but already he could feel its effect on his mind and body. Jack had to fight to stay positive.

"Do not lose heart, children," Elion called from beside him. Even beneath the slithering darkness, her skin sparkled like diamonds.

Alexia brought her winged fox closer. Jack had recently learned that Alexia Dreager was his sister, though he hadn't found the right time to tell her yet. He'd grown up with an older brother, Parker. But he knew now that Parker was not his real brother. For a reason he didn't understand, Parker and Alexia had been switched at birth.

"The Assassin only has the power you give him. Even this darkness will not touch you if you don't allow it." Elion spoke loudly to be heard over the wind.

"But what is it? How could the Assassin possibly black out the sky?" Jack asked.

"It is the Assassin's Shadow. It is his essence. It is fear and hatred, pride and jealousy. And those who bathe in its darkness must fight to stay pure." Elion's eyes shifted to white gold. "I don't know how he created it, but it was spoken of in the prophecy as his greatest weapon. I am afraid the end is near. The world won't be able to stand beneath this darkness for more than a few days."

Now her eyes were deep maroon. "Take heart, Jack Staples and Alexia Dreager. The size of the enemy is far less important than the warriors' strength of heart and will. No matter how great the darkness becomes, you must allow your lights to shine. There can be no room for fear."

"But I am afraid," Jack said. "How can I not fear when everyone I know and love could be hurt or killed?"

"You misunderstand. I am also afraid. I fear for you and Alexia." Elion shifted her gaze to Alexia. "And I fear for the Awakened. Will they be strong enough to stand against the hordes of darkness? But I do not fear the Assassin, for he only has the power that we give him. And I do not fear his followers, for they are not evil; they are simply deceived. While the two of you still live, there is hope for this world."

A shiver pricked across Jack's skin. Between one breath and the next, the world had become … pure! The slithering darkness still obscured the sky, yet the feeling of misery was gone. "What just happened?" Jack looked around.

"The air is so clean!" Alexia gasped.

Jack looked in wonder at the valley below. Every tree stood strong and tall, and the world was filled with color. Even without the light of the sun, the flowered fields and rich grass were beautiful.

"Ah! It seems we have arrived at last." Elion smiled. "It is good to be in an Oasis again! In many ways they feel similar to the world where I was born. Yet I cannot stay with you any longer."

"What?" Jack and Alexia said at the same time.

"You can't leave! We just got here," Jack said. "Isn't the Shadow Army still following?"

"Yes, but there is something I must attend to." Elion turned and flew backward as she spoke. "The Last Battle has come, and in every corner of the world, in every city, town, and village, the fighting will be fierce. On every mountaintop and in every valley, the world is raging against itself." Elion's eyes shifted between crimson and black.

"But the true battle lies with the two of you. Whether or not you are successful in defeating the Assassin is the only thing that matters. So I go to raise an army to fight beside you." Elion turned to face forward again. "So long, Jack Staples. Remember that no matter how skilled a Blades Master you become, your sword is merely a tool. Your truest weapon lies in your heart. And so long,

Alexia Dreager. Remember that no matter how lonely you may feel, you are never alone. You are surrounded by friends who love you very much."

Without another word, Elion turned and flew back in the direction they had come. Jack looked at Alexia. She shrugged, and then her fox dropped to dart between the trees far below.

Jack inhaled deeply, filling his lungs with pure oxygen. Whatever evil was happening in the world, inside the Oasis, there was only good. Just being here made him feel better. The place radiated energy. He still needed sleep, but his mind was working quicker, and the aches in his muscles were beginning to fade. His winged panther circled down and landed in a small clearing. Jack stepped down and patted her.

When they'd left the cavern, Jack told Mrs. Dumphry of his new memory. She'd listened until he was done and for a long time hadn't said a word. Finally she'd smiled and said, "You have come up with a very good plan." Before Jack could respond, she'd flown ahead. Now that they'd arrived at the Oasis, Jack was more nervous than ever.

Within seconds, the Oasis was stirring like a kicked anthill. Everywhere he looked, people ran this way and that, carrying armloads of supplies as animals darted between them. A feeling of desperation settled around Jack as he watched. *Can they escape in time, or will every one of them die today?*

"Child, I need you to go pick up that tree."

Jack turned to see Mrs. Dumphry climbing down from her elephant. She stood and placed her fists in the small of her back and cracked it loudly.

"You want me to pick up a tree?" he said slowly.

"Yes. We will need that tree if we are to save these people."

"I don't understand. How can I pick up a tree?"

Mrs. Dumphry snorted. "You can't, of course. It's a ridiculous request."

"They why did you just—"

"A true leader does not carry what is not meant for him. Try and you'll be crushed as sure as a feather beneath a mountain. You are not responsible for what happens to these people. I suggest you start working on what you are responsible for and leave the rest to those who are meant to carry it." Mrs. Dumphry's birdlike eyes never blinked as she spoke.

"But I don't know if it will work," Jack admitted. "What if I'm not strong enough? I wasn't trying to come up with a plan; I was just telling you what I remembered. Except I don't even know if I remember! What if I try and nothing happens?"

"There is no shame in trying and failing. But to never try for fear of failure is the greatest shame on earth."

"It's not that I won't try," Jack said. "I'll do my best, I promise. But if ... if I fail, every one of us will die."

"Well, then"—Mrs. Dumphry winked—"I suppose you had better not fail." She chuckled as if she'd made a grand joke, then turned and stalked toward the gathering crowd.

Jack hadn't noticed the hundreds of Awakened arriving behind them as they spoke. It looked as if every member of the Oasis had crowded in the clearing. All were laden with bedrolls, blankets, food; and by the looks on their faces, they were afraid.

Jack tried to shove down the anxiety rising inside him. He knew what was about to happen. The Assassin's minions would descend on this place of beauty and peace, and unless these people were able to sneak away, every one of them would be captured or killed. As for the Oasis, he didn't know what would happen, but he was sure it would be bad.

Mrs. Dumphry stepped forward. "My name is Mrs. Dumphry, and you should know that ten thousand Shadow Souled are on their way and will arrive soon."

Whimpering children clutched parents as adults shifted uncomfortably, yet none spoke. All eyes stayed glued on Mrs. Dumphry.

"You are not who you used to be," she continued. "You are members of the Awakened and far from helpless. Three hundred leagues to the east, you will find a Great Oasis where the Awakened are gathering by the hundreds of thousands. Many of you have felt it in your hearts, a tugging, that feeling of something drawing you away. Just as that feeling brought you here, it will guide you in all things. It is one of the ways the Author communicates with us. If you feel it now, it is because he is calling you to the Great Oasis."

Many in the crowd nodded as if they had indeed felt something.

"Your journey will be treacherous, but be strong and have courage." Mrs. Dumphry walked through the gathered crowd. "Look out for each other. The world has become far more dangerous than it once was. Do not give in to despair. In the midst of darkness, you are the light. But be wary! Just as this Oasis stands with you, you will find Quagmires that have joined the Assassin. No matter how far you must travel to go around them, do not under any circumstances enter a Quagmire. To do so would be a quick and brutal death. Now stay strong and keep together!"

"Does this mean you won't be coming with us?" A small, shaggy-haired man stepped forward. "I'd hoped you might lead us there."

"No." Mrs. Dumphry shook her head. "You will be far safer if we don't travel with you." She placed a hand on the man's shoulder.

"Both of the Children of Prophecy are with us. The Shadow Souled will not stop until they are captured or dead."

Gasps erupted from the gathered crowd. Every eye fixed on the four children—Wild, Alexia, Arthur, and Jack. The crowd was clearly trying to ascertain which two were the Children of Prophecy. Each face showed a mixture of fear and wonder.

The prophecy says we will destroy them. It says we will destroy the whole world. Jack shared an uneasy look with Alexia. *They're right to be afraid.* Yet the prophecy also said they would defeat the Assassin and save the world. It didn't make a lick of sense, and even the Council of Seven didn't pretend to understand it.

"We will stay here and draw the enemy's attention while you flee," Mrs. Dumphry continued. "If our plan works"—she met Jack's eyes—"the dark servants will not be able to follow where we go. Now there's no time to dally. Off with you."

Mrs. Dumphry began talking quietly to Andreal. For a long moment, the gathered crowd stood unmoving as if unsure they'd been dismissed. Finally the small fellow shook his head and began shouting instructions.

Jack studied Mrs. Dumphry. She had been his teacher back in Ballylesson and was the oldest woman he'd ever met. *No,* he remembered, *she's the oldest woman who ever lived.* Mrs. Dumphry's wiry gray hair was pulled back in a large bun, and her petite frame appeared far more brittle than it truly was.

As the crowd dispersed, Jack tried to suppress his anxiety. Everything that was about to happen hinged on the shadow of a memory. He had no other way to explain it, but what he was going to try had not happened, though he still remembered it. At least he had the *feeling* of remembering it. His stomach churned as he walked toward a nearby tree. When he sat, he startled as the grass thickened beneath him.

Mrs. Dumphry had told them about the Oases that were forming all throughout the world. Yet until he arrived, he hadn't fully believed her. Just as the humans and Clear Eyes were gathering, so too was the rest of the world. The Oases were gathering places for followers of the Author. The trees and grass, the bugs and reptiles, the air itself would fight alongside the Awakened in the Last Battle. Inside the Oasis, every stone and blade of grass, every tree, rock, and grain of dirt stood defiant against the Assassin.

Jack eyed the grass warily before leaning his head against the tree. He breathed in pure oxygen, and the wind danced along his skin, blowing the aches from his body. It was so peaceful, it was almost possible to forget the slithering darkness in the sky above. Jack closed his eyes and tried to clear his mind. *I need to think!*

When he opened his eyes again, Jack wanted to scream. He'd fallen asleep without meaning to, and in the short time he'd slept, the Oasis had changed. *Not yet!* The thought tore through him. *I'm not ready!* The grass beneath him had begun to brown, and a sickly sweet smell filled the air. Jack scrambled to his feet. None of the hundreds of people he'd seen were there, and only a few of the Clear Eyes remained.

Mrs. Dumphry, Wild, and Andreal stood a short distance away, talking quietly. Jack sprinted over. "Why didn't anyone wake me?" he gasped.

"You were not needed," Mrs. Dumphry said. "Did you sleep well?"

Jack gaped.

"I hope so, because your time has come, and we will soon put this plan of yours to the test."

Again Jack wanted to scream. "I don't even know if I can take more than one! I'm not ready. It isn't even a memory; it's more like a dream I can barely remember!" The wind picked up, smelling of rot and decay.

"If I threw an egg in the air and expected it to fly, who would be at fault when it crashed to the ground: me or the egg?" Mrs. Dumphry said happily.

Jack blinked. His teacher rarely said anything that wasn't confusing. "You," he said irritably. "It would be your fault if the egg broke."

"You are correct! All things happen in their time. You are an egg no longer. You have become a bird, and it is time to fly."

Jack's eyebrows climbed as he tried to make sense of it. "But I—"

Mrs. Dumphry held up her hand. "It is time." She turned to Wild. "Wake the others and have them form a circle in the center of the clearing. Young Jack will tell us what to do from there."

Wild nodded, then ran off to fetch the others.

Jack tried to swallow his doubt. He glanced toward Mrs. Dumphry, but she and Andreal were already walking toward the clearing. The Oasis was fading quickly, changing into something dark and menacing. *It's going to be destroyed.* Jack's thoughts were frantic as the trees pitted with rot and decay and the air thinned. It was hard to breathe.

He ran to the center of the clearing as little whirlwinds formed and spun wildly, tearing at the withering grass. Even as his friends joined him, trees began snapping like twigs, crashing to the ground.

"The Oasis is turning much faster than I expected. I would suggest you do not dally, child." Mrs. Dumphry winked at Jack.

Distant howls, screeches, and roars sounded from every direction. The army of the Shadow Souled had come. Every living thing that refused to follow the Assassin was being utterly destroyed, or worse. Mrs. Dumphry had told him that parts of the Oasis might switch allegiances. In order to stay alive, trees, grass, animals, even the air itself might choose to become agents of evil.

"You can do this," Alexia said.

Arthur was slightly paler than everyone else. "I've been meaning to ask …" Arthur said, "what happens if only some of us go back? You know? I don't want to get left here. And if we all do go back, how long before we come back again? You know, back to now, but not here. And is it possible that some of us might get stuck back then and not make it back to now? If so, could you go back again and get the ones who'd been left in the past and bring them back, but to a different place, you know?"

"Arthur!" Alexia shouted. "You're not helping."

"Right," Arthur said, quickly patting Jack on the shoulder. "Sorry. I'm sure you'll do just fine."

Jack tried to ignore his friends. *Keep your mind on what you're doing!* He breathed deep. "All right!" He yelled to be heard over the wind and snapping trees. "Everyone grab hands and hold on tight. No matter what happens, don't let go of the hand next to you until we arrive."

"What happens if we let go?" Arthur asked.

"I don't know, but I think it'll be bad," Jack said.

There were six in the circle—Mrs. Dumphry, Andreal, Wild, Alexia, Arthur, and Jack. He tried not to think about the Oasis as the smell of death thickened and a heavy rain began to fall.

"Jack Staples"—Mrs. Dumphry's voice cut through the chaos— "you are stronger than you can possibly comprehend."

Jack nodded, trying to ignore the crumbling landscape. *Where is it?* He listened with all his heart, desperate to hear his note, but there was nothing. *Where are the bells? Where is the ring of Time?*

The wind whipped the rain, rocketing it in every direction, leaving Jack half blind. Arthur screamed as the ground began to soften. Jack would have screamed too if he hadn't been so scared. All six Awakened sank downward in the newly forming quicksand.

Come on! The trees that remained standing had become menacing things of thick thorns and spindly vines, and they were moving into the clearing! A spout of fire erupted from a sinkhole just behind Arthur.

"I do no mean to be complaining," Andreal boomed, "but if we do be leaving, it might be best if we be going now!" The giant's fiery orange hair and black beard were slick with muddied rain.

"The animals are turning!" Arthur screamed.

Jack had already noticed a few. Throughout the forest, animals were stopping. Many of the beasts dropped and began thrashing about; a moment later they rose again with pink eyes and frothy snouts. Yet many of the Clear Eyes grew bolder as they began circling the Awakened protectively.

Jack met Mrs. Dumphry's eyes, but she merely watched him, a small smile parting her lips. He was beginning to think it would be impossible to hear anything. They were now thigh-deep in the muck and still sinking.

"What are you waiting for?" Arthur shouted.

Jack coughed as metallic vapor appeared in the center of the circle. Whatever the vapor was, it was thickening. "Come on!" he screamed. "Please? I need to hear it!" Suddenly, exploding from somewhere deep in his chest, Jack heard his note. Never before had it been so loud or so powerful.

Jack let the sound fill every part of him. The melody wove around him, each beat matching the rhythm of his heart. It was a fantastical song that reverberated throughout the clearing, wrapping each member of the Awakened. Along with the cadence came a feeling of absolute peace. Even as the mist congealed in front of him, Jack fully embraced his note. And in a flash of light, Jack and his friends exploded from the clearing, flying backward through the air.

Chapter 3

A MEMORABLE—SORT OF—BEGINNING

Jack and his friends dropped like stones. It had worked! He'd taken everyone with him. He hadn't known it was possible to time travel with someone until he'd done it with the Assassin a few days earlier. This was too good to be true.

Flying through time had changed for Jack. Until recently he'd always felt dizzy and confused when he arrived somewhere. But when he flew through time now, he had far more control. Now he arrived alert and energized. The group neared the ground, and Jack slowed their descent, landing them softly.

I did it. He sighed. He'd taken everyone safely away from the army of the Shadow Souled. At the moment he didn't care if he'd picked the right time or place. All that mattered was that they were safe! He turned his gaze to the valley below. The sun touched the horizon, bathing the world in golden light. He closed his eyes, letting the warmth sink into him. They were in a time before the Assassin's Shadow had swallowed the world.

In the valley was a gathering of colorful covered wagons. At the center of the gathering stood an enormous tent and several smaller tents and cages. Jack felt his heart quicken as he eyed the hundreds of people walking among them. *Is she really there?* He could barely stand still, he was so excited. Now that they were safely in the past, the hard part was over. The rest of his plan would be nothing but magical.

"You did it," Alexia said. "I wasn't sure I believed you until now. But we're really here." Her eyes were locked on the tents.

"I think I picked the right night," Jack said, feeling suddenly nervous. He glanced at the clear sky. "It's supposed to rain soon, remember?"

"I don't remember much from that night. I woke up in a mud puddle with a raging headache."

"Well done!" Mrs. Dumphry clapped a hand on Jack's back. "Well done, indeed." She turned to address the others. "Yet I am afraid we may not be as safe as I had hoped."

"What do you mean?" Jack asked. "They couldn't possibly follow us here, could they?"

"No, the Shadow Army has been left safely in the present. But that mist you saw just before we left was the Odius that Elion told

us about. The creature is nearly as deadly as the Assassin, and as far
as we know, it's impossible to kill."

"But we're here. How are we not safe?" Arthur asked. "We're
in the past!"

"Besides being a master of death, an Odius can read a Soulprint
and imitate it. If the beast arrived in time, it may eventually figure
out where and when we are. Given enough time, there is a chance it
could follow. I doubt it could bring more than a handful of Shadow
Souled with it, but an Odius is an army unto itself."

"So what now?" Jack asked.

"Nothing changes. We do what we came here for. If the creature arrives, we flee and make sure it follows. This is not a battle
we can win, especially here. And if it does come, we cannot afford
to leave it in the past." Mrs. Dumphry's eyes locked on the tents
below. "We must act quickly and get out. The fate of the world rests
on what we accomplish today."

"You really don't mind if I talk to her?" Jack thought Mrs.
Dumphry would be against this part of his plan.

"You must do exactly as you remember. Nothing more and
nothing less."

Jack turned to Arthur. "Alexia and I will make sure you have
enough time. Just be sure he doesn't see you."

Arthur nodded.

"Off with you," Mrs. Dumphry said.

Jack and Alexia broke into a run. As they neared the wagons,
Alexia separated and ran toward the opposite end. She seemed
to know where she could sneak in. *This is it,* Jack thought as he
approached the entry.

The colorful wagons had been circled round to act as a make-shift wall. Hundreds of people stood in a queue, entering through a gap between two wagons. Jack pulled his hood low and joined the queue, placing five pence in the hand of a large, rough-looking man. He walked past a number of cages and corrals filled with exotic animals, yet he ignored them all. The sun dipped below the horizon as his eyes hungrily scanned the crowd.

There! Jack stopped, suddenly breathless. His mother stood just a few paces away. She was even more beautiful than he remembered. Beside her was his older brother, Parker, and a younger Jack Staples. His mother's hands rested on both boys' shoulders as they gaped at a grizzly sleeping in a cage. *My mother is here, and she's alive!* Jack didn't bother trying to keep the tears from his eyes. He wanted to run to her, to wrap his arms around her, but he made himself wait.

Where is she? He rocked on his heels as he waited for Alexia.

Parker stepped away from the bear and walked over to another enclosure. "Mother, come look," he called. "It's a crocodile!"

Parker leaned heavily against a wooden fence, staring wide-eyed into the pen.

"Shall we go see it?" Jack's mother asked the younger Jack.

"Can I wait just a little while?"

"Of course you can. It's your birthday after all!" Megan Staples said as she ruffled his hair.

Jack spotted Alexia approaching from the opposite side. The timing couldn't have been more perfect. She'd found a drab, brown cape from somewhere and wore it atop her crimson cloak. As Jack's mother stepped away, Alexia sauntered over to the younger Jack and began talking.

Eleven months and twenty-eight days earlier

Jack Staples walked between his mother and his older brother, Parker. He'd never been more excited in his life. Today was his eleventh birthday, and his mother had taken them to the circus to celebrate. He'd never been to a circus before and couldn't believe his luck. A sign strung between two of the tents read "A Menagerie of Marvels and Wonders."

A man riding a unicycle and juggling five sticks of fire wheeled past, followed by a clown walking on very tall stilts. When Jack spotted the grizzly bear, his jaw dropped. He let go of his mother and Parker's hands and ran over to get a closer look. A moment later, Parker arrived beside him, and Jack felt his mother's hand on his shoulder.

"It's pretty fearsome, isn't it, my boy?" she said.

"It's huge!" Jack couldn't keep from rocking on his heels.

Parker darted away to look into the next enclosure, but Jack was far too interested in the bear to leave so soon. He'd wanted to see a bear for as long as he could remember.

"Mother, come look!" Jack turned to see Parker leaning against a wooden fence and pointing. "It's a crocodile!"

"Shall we go see it?" Jack's mother asked.

"Can I wait just a little while?"

"Of course you can. It's your birthday after all!" She ruffled his hair, then went to join Parker at the crocodile enclosure.

"Amazing, isn't it?"

Jack turned to see a girl standing next to him. She had bright-green eyes and was probably two or three years older. Her raven-black hair hung loose at her shoulders, and she wore a brown cloak. The girl was absolutely beautiful.

"It is amazing!" Jack agreed, feeling his cheeks grow warm.

"Do you want to see the elephant?" The girl moved in close and whispered in his ear. "I'll let you pet him if you come with me now."

"Yes, please!" Jack jumped up and down. "Can I bring my mother and brother?"

The girl put her fingers to her lips in a shushing motion. "No," she whispered, "I can sneak only one person in, and I've picked you. But we need to go right away. We'll be back in just a minute, I promise. Your mother won't even know you're gone!"

Jack glanced at his mother and Parker. "All right," he said, barely able to contain his excitement. He'd always dreamed of embarking on an adventure!

"You'll need to leave your coat, though." The girl thumbed his collar. "Elephants hate the color green. Hang it on this fence post, and you can get it when you come back."

Jack unbuttoned his coat and did as she asked. *It's sure good she told me,* he thought. *It could have been really bad if I'd kept it on!*

He took the girl's hand as she led him past the ostrich pen and under a rope that had been strung up to block people from crossing.

"I don't think we're meant to be back here," he said as they passed a number of colorful wagons. Far fewer lanterns hung on this side of the rope, and there were no patrons except Jack and the girl.

"Really? Whatever gave you that idea?"

Jack couldn't tell if she was making fun. "I think the rope was there to keep people out," he whispered.

"Oh, I doubt it." The girl grinned. "I bet it's just for decoration. I think it looked rather nice, don't you?"

Jack opened his mouth to disagree but still couldn't tell if she was teasing, so he closed it again. The girl stopped beside a large red wagon and pulled out a stool from underneath a door in the side. She stepped up on the stool and yanked hard on the handle. The door opened as soft lantern light spilled out. She winked at Jack, then disappeared inside.

Jack's heart pounded as he followed her. He'd only seen pictures of elephants before and hadn't believed they were this big. The beast's head brushed the ceiling! It wrapped its trunk around the girl's waist, and she leaned into it and whispered in the elephant's ear. When she finally turned her attention to Jack, there were tears in her eyes.

"His name is Ollie, and he was one of my very best friends," she said as she rubbed Ollie's trunk.

"You work at the circus?"

"I used to, but I quit after tonight." The girl flashed a toothy smile. "I wanted to introduce you to Ollie as a birthday present. Happy birthday, Jack Staples." She stepped past him and leaped from the wagon. "Now, we best be getting back to your mother before she starts to worry."

Outside the wagon, Jack stopped. "How do you know my name? And how did you know it was my birthday?"

"Oh, I know lots of things about you! But don't worry, we'll meet soon enough."

"Didn't we just meet?" Jack was beginning to wonder if the girl might be a bit loony. "Who are you?"

"My name is Al—" She stopped, then offered a roguish grin. "My name is Blade. Now, we had best be going. We don't want you to miss the show!"

"Oi! You two, wait right there!" A girl in a crimson cloak stepped out of a large green wagon a short distance away. "What were you doing to my elephant? How dare you come back here!"

Blade grabbed Jack's hand and began to run. "We'd better hide," she said. "That one's got a real temper on her!"

Eleven months and twenty-eight days later

When Alexia ran off with the younger Jack, the memory solidified in Jack's mind. She was about to introduce him to Ollie. And she was about to tease him, a lot. He grinned at the absurdity of it. It was so strange to be remembering things as they happened. The moment they were on their way, Jack darted over and climbed into the coat the younger Jack had left. He was surprised to find it tight in the shoulders. *Have I really grown so much in just a year?* He hurried to his mother and wrapped his arms around her, doing his best to hold back the tears.

She smiled at him. "What is it, my Jack? What's going on?"

"I've missed you so much!" he blurted. *So much for being subtle!* But he didn't care. From the corner of his eye, he saw Parker dart off to the next enclosure.

"I didn't go anywhere, silly! Parker and I have been watching the crocodile. Have you seen it yet?"

"I love you, Mother," Jack whispered, not letting go. "I just want to make sure you know."

"Of course I do! But I always like hearing it!" She knelt in front of him and thumbed the hem of his coat. "This is getting tight on you. I suppose I shall have to make you another now that you are eleven years old! You're growing like a sprout." She stood and scanned the crowd. "Now, shall we gather your brother and find a seat for the show? I hear it's spectacular."

"Yes, Mother," Jack said, feeling fresh tears forming. "But I want to say thank you!"

"For what?" She stopped and knelt again. "What's going on, Jack? Is there something you're not telling me?"

Jack exhaled, calming himself. "No, I just want to say thank you for all of it. You're always looking out for us. You're always there for us, and I don't know if I ever thanked you."

"What else is a mother to do?" She pulled Jack close and hugged him. "I love you. You know that, right? And I'm desperately proud of you." She stood again. "Now, where has Parker gone?"

Jack took a deep breath. He knew he had to leave before the younger Jack returned. But he couldn't make himself move.

"Do you see him?" His mother scanned the surrounding crowd. "I told him not to wander off."

Jack shook his head. He was afraid if he spoke, he would burst into tears. He fixed the picture in his mind, his mother standing there looking for Parker. Jack knew Arthur must still be busy with Parker. That was the true reason they had come. Jack and Alexia were merely keeping the younger Jack and his mother busy.

"Ah, there he is, next to the ostrich pen. Come, my boy. Let's collect him and get inside."

Jack trailed behind his mother, then darted over to the fence post. The younger Jack was already there, searching the ground for the coat. Jack quickly climbed out of it, then turned his back to the younger Jack, pretending to study the grizzly.

"Is this yours?" he asked, holding the coat out behind him.

"Oh yes, it is!" the younger Jack said excitedly. "I was looking for that." He snatched the cloak, then ran off to find his mother. "Thank you!" he called back as he ran.

Jack let out a relieved breath as he turned to see Alexia grinning at him.

"What's so funny?" he asked.

"You were so cute!" Alexia burst out laughing. "I wanted to pinch your cheeks the whole time."

"Oi! You two! Stop right there. You're going to tell me what you were doing to my elephant, you bull-brained ninnies!" A younger Alexia was stalking angrily toward them.

"At least I was cute," Jack said. "You've always been scary!" Both children laughed as they ran from the younger Alexia. *All we need to do now is find Arthur and get out of here!* Jack was so happy, he could barely contain himself. He'd been able to talk to his mother one last time, to say the things he wanted to say.

He began to laugh as they ran past the exotic animals and gawking patrons. So long as Arthur had been able to give Parker the Poet's Coffer, their mission would be a complete success.

Chapter 4

SIBLINGS

Alexia was giddy with excitement. The circus had been her home for almost six years, and she'd loved every minute of it. The night the circus burned to the ground had been devastating. These animals were her best friends, and many had been killed or injured in the fire.

With everything that had happened since, Alexia never dreamed she'd see the circus again. But this was better than she could have hoped. She was able to see it as it truly was, before the fire. To top it off, Jack had taken them to the past, where the world had yet to go mad. The Assassin's Shadow had not swallowed the sky, the weather was normal, and there was no fear of a sudden earthquake or tornado springing up.

She'd wanted to kiss Jack when she heard his plan. He'd seen the Poet's Coffer before, when he saw a vision of his brother running away from a great darkness, clutching a wooden box.

Alexia was so thrilled to be back, she didn't care what Jack had seen. And she didn't want to go back to the future, where the world seemed to be crumbling. Her life in the circus had been carefree. She hadn't realized how much she missed it. Spending her days with the animals and her evenings performing before jubilant crowds had been a magnificent life.

Alexia darted behind the zebra corral, followed closely by Jack. They hid in the shadows as the younger Alexia ran past. It was crazy to be back in time, hiding from herself. "She won't keep searching for us," Alexia whispered. "The show's about to begin."

"We need to find Arthur and get out of here," Jack whispered.

Alexia's heart sank. She knew he was right. They needed to defeat the Assassin. More importantly, she needed to free her friends and find her mother. But she wanted to stay in the past.

"There." Jack pointed at the giraffe enclosure near the entry. Arthur was milling about with his hands in his pockets, trying to look natural. Alexia could see Ben, the money taker, sitting at the entry. She'd never spent much time with the man but had always liked him. Ben had a keen eye for spotting trouble. More than once she'd seen him arrive just in time to break up a fight before it could begin.

"You wait here," Alexia whispered. "I'll get Arthur, and we can leave the back way." Before Jack could respond, Alexia shrugged out of her brown cloak and stepped into the light. "Grand fine evening," she said as she glanced at the gathering clouds.

Ben blinked, then glanced at the circus tent. "Aren't ye supposed to be gettin' ready?"

"What are they going to do, start without me?" Alexia grinned.
"I came to collect my cousin." She glanced at Arthur, who was watching nervously. "Well, Cousin, are you going to stand there all day?
We can't keep the good people waiting."

"Yes, Cousin," Arthur said. "It was wonderful of you to invite me."

"You be careful in there." Ben grimaced. "There's something mighty strange about tonight. It's almost as if the shadows …"

"As if what?"

"Never ye mind. I'll keep ye safe. Just be careful in there, Blade."

Alexia leaped up and spun her body around in a double-twisted backflip. She landed with arms wide and a rueful grin. The few patrons not yet in the tent clapped their hands in delight. "It'll take more than shadows to knock me off balance!" She gave a flourish of her crimson cloak.

Ben nodded, then tipped his hat and turned to stare into the darkness. "Ye better go. I don't want Master Julius to have me head for making ye late."

Alexia grabbed Arthur's hand, then walked toward Jack.

"You're the right Alexia, right?" Arthur whispered. "I mean, it's really you from the future and not you from the past?"

Alexia sighed.

"That went well," Arthur said. "I put the coffer and Mrs. Dumphry's note in Parker's pocket while he was gawking at the rhino. He didn't notice a thing. But I've been wondering … Why didn't you or Alexia do it? Why did all three of us need to be here?"

"I don't know," Jack said, "but that's what I remembered, so that's what we did." He placed an arm around Arthur's shoulders. "Right, then, should we go back to the others?"

"Not yet," Alexia said. "I want to see something first."

"We should get back as soon as possible," Jack said. "You heard Mrs. Dumphry. We need to get out of here quickly in case the Odius comes."

"You can go if you like, but I'm staying a little longer." Alexia snuck around toward the entrance of the great tent.

"What is she doing?" Arthur whispered.

"I don't know," Jack said, "but we can't leave her."

By the time they rounded the tent, Alexia was already standing atop a large covered wagon that had been positioned tight against the side of the circus tent. Jack began to climb as Alexia pulled a small flap of the thick canvas aside and peeked in. Jack hoisted himself up beside her and looked inside. The crowd roared as the younger Alexia walked into the tent and threw her arms wide.

"I'm sorry I didn't cry when she died," Alexia said, and Jack realized she was watching his mother. "I don't think I had any tears left." She scrubbed at the wetness on her cheeks. "You had a really amazing mother, Jack." She met his eyes and smiled. "And I'm proud to have known her, even for just a short time."

Jack felt as if he'd been punched in the gut. "There's something I have to tell you," he said without thinking. "She's …" He was surprised at the wetness in his own eyes. "It's just that … well, I didn't know how to tell you before, but she's your mother, too. You and my brother, Parker, were switched at birth. I don't know why, but I'm sure of it. Time told me when I was in the Forbidden Garden. You are my sister."

Alexia's smile faded and she stared at Jack as though she'd never seen him before.

Arthur Greaves hoisted himself up. "I really think we need to go," he said. "Mrs. Dumphry and the others are waiting."

Jack's breath caught at the dangerous look in Alexia's eyes. The two children sat staring at each other, completely unmoving.

"Did you hear what I said?" Arthur placed a hand on Jack's shoulder. "We need to go. It's not safe." Rain began to fall, and still Alexia didn't say a word. "Wait, what did I miss?" Arthur leaned in close, studying his friends.

"You've known this for days, and you choose to tell me now?" Alexia said.

"I didn't know how to tell you," Jack said. "I thought … I don't know. I should have said something earlier, but I didn't know how."

"I'm not sure what's happening here," Arthur said, "but isn't the tent about to start on fire? This isn't the best place to have this conversation. Let's continue talking after we get back to the future."

Inside the tent, the younger Alexia stepped on the rope between the two platforms as both lions roared loudly. The tumblers spun, the crowd gasped, and all three children sat in the thickening rain. *She's right*, Jack thought. *I should have told her.*

The covered wagon shook violently. Jack looked down to see a gorilla bounce off the side and lumber into the darkness.

"What on earth is that doing out of its cage?" Arthur's eyes followed the gorilla. "And what is that?" He pointed into the darkness.

Jack wiped rain from his eyes, searching the darkness. His heart sank. At least thirty Shadow Souled were stalking between the wagons. They moved slowly, stopping every few paces to sniff the air. There were a number of Oriax, a Shadule, and something Jack didn't recognize—a beastly creature with rippling black, metallic skin. Every few steps it contorted into the shape of something recognizable, then twisted again into something monstrous. It was a black lion, then a monster, a fanged rabbit, a spiked turtle, and a monster again. The creature never kept its shape for long, and the only constant were the pale eyes ringing its head.

"What is it?" Jack breathed. The monster became a spider, a child, a monster, a horse.

"I told you we should have gone," Arthur whimpered. The metallic creature had stopped near the grizzly enclosure. The poor bear cowered on the far side of the cage. The monster contorted into the shape of a wolf and smelled the ground.

A ball of fire shot through the night to explode against the wolf's metallic side. The creature snarled even as it dissipated into a cloud of black mist. A rather large blackbird that had been perched on a nearby fence post screeched and flew away. Jack's eyes locked on the shrieking bird as it rocketed through an open flap near the top of the great circus tent.

The mist congealed as Mrs. Dumphry stepped out of the shadows and sent a spiderweb of fire into the Oriax. Andreal's ax and Wild's bow cleaved a bloody path through the dark servants.

Jack watched the mist gel into the monster once again. The rippling creature ignored the battle, stalking toward the entrance of the tent. Mrs. Dumphry was too busy fighting the winged Shadule to see what the monster was doing.

"That must be the Odius," Alexia said. The beast had become a lion and was padding slowly forward. Inside the tent, hundreds of men, women, and children gasped and cheered, unaware of what was happening just outside.

The Odius stood before the entrance of the tent in the form of a monster. It sniffed the air and snarled, its metallic skin rippling.

"It smells you!" Alexia gasped.

"Then why is it walking toward the—" Jack realized what was happening. The Odius smelled the Jack from the past.

"We have to stop it!" His throat was desert dry. *What happens if the younger me gets killed? Do I die as well?*

He leaped from the wagon and landed on his knees in the thickening mud, then lunged to his feet as Alexia landed deftly beside him. Arthur tried to climb down but lost his balance. But Jack's eyes were on the black snake that slithered into the circus tent. He sprinted after it, but when he entered the tent, he skidded to a stop.

He stood in warm lantern light, wiping muddy rain from his eyes. Alexia stopped beside him as the younger Alexia at the center of the tent walked along the tightrope. With each step the crowd gasped in wonder. Above it all, the terrified blackbird slammed itself into the tent ceiling again and again.

There! Jack saw the snake slither beneath the bleachers. He scanned the crowd and found his mother, brother, and the younger Jack. Their eyes were on the spectacle at the center of the tent. The lions, tumblers, and the younger Alexia demanded the attention of everyone but the two children from the future.

Jack sprinted toward where he'd seen the Odius disappear, then dove beneath the seats. His heart sank. The creature was already nearing the younger Jack.

Jack was dimly aware of the crowd gasping from the other side of the bleachers. He half crawled, half ran after the rippling snake, though he was sure he wouldn't be able to catch it in time. *And what would I do if I caught it?* It was a cold thought. Mrs. Dumphry had said the creature was impossible to kill. Yet still he pursued it. He couldn't just stand there and watch himself die.

Jack could see his own feet on the other side of the bleachers. The younger Jack stood alongside his brother and mother as the crowd bellowed. The Odius didn't slow as it neared the seat, but rippled again, contorting into a sleek jaguar.

I'm too late! I didn't even get to say good-bye to Father. The jaguar leaped at the younger Jack's legs with teeth bared. "No!" Jack shouted. The Odius was in midair when something very peculiar happened. Just as the creature's nose bumped into the younger Jack's leg, Jack heard his note and felt a sudden burst of wind. The Odius rocketed backward, howling in surprise. Jack braced himself, but a split second before the Odius crashed into him, the creature disappeared in an explosion of light.

Jack stood for a long moment, totally perplexed. The crowd thundered as the tightrope-walking Alexia spread her crimson cloak wide. Jack could see her from between the younger Jack's legs.

"That was weird," Alexia said breathlessly. "Did you do that?"

"I don't know," Jack said. "I think so, but I have no idea how." The children stood side by side watching the younger Alexia and not saying a word.

"You had no right to keep it from me," Alexia said.

Jack turned to face her.

"You came back here to hide the Poet's Coffer and say good-bye to your mother. But you never gave me the chance to say good-bye."

"I—" Jack's throat caught. "You're right. And I'm sorry. I don't know what else to say." Jack could see Parker holding his hand in the shape of a lion's claw. The show was over, and the nightmare was about to begin. "We need to go," he said carefully. "Beast and Killer are about to escape, and we need to find the others." The two great lions crouched low on the sandy ground, their eyes glued to the shrieking blackbird.

Alexia turned to peek up through the crack in the bleachers. Jack also looked. His mother watched her boys with a look of pure love. Jack grabbed Alexia's hand and met her eyes. She nodded, then both children turned and ran toward the tent entrance. They crawled from beneath the bleachers into the pouring rain and almost ran into Arthur and Mrs. Dumphry. Inside the tent, horrified screams erupted. Jack turned to see the younger Alexia lying on her back between the two beasts.

"Where is the Odius?" Mrs. Dumphry's voice was tight.

"I don't know," Jack said. "But it's not here. It disappeared in a burst of light just before it attacked me. I mean, before it attacked the other me."

Mrs. Dumphry's eyebrows climbed. "Thank the Author. We will discuss it later, but we've been here far too long already. We must get back to the future before something else goes wrong."

Screaming men, women, and children poured from the tent. The lions roared as they stalked through the terrified crowd. A man stumbled into a lamppost, snapping it in two. The glass cylinder shattered, sending fiery oil onto the tent walls. Jack and his friends ran into the darkness as the circus tent erupted in flames.

Alexia's heart broke. She ran alongside Jack and the others, leaving her circus friends—and leaving Megan Staples. *Could she really be*

my mother? The thought tumbled through her mind. She was furious with Jack for keeping it from her, but could he be mistaken?

Andreal and Wild were waiting in the trees. Both had weapons in hand and were standing back to back as if expecting an attack at any moment. Rain poured down and lightning streaked the sky. In the valley below, the circus tent sent flames reaching into the darkness.

"Child," Mrs. Dumphry said to Jack, "you must take us back to the present, yet not to where we left. Bring us to the Great Oasis I told you about."

"I'll do my best," Jack said, "but I don't know if it works like that. I've never been to the Great Oasis, and I don't know where it is. But I'll try."

"It is all I ask."

"Everyone grab hands and don't let go!" Jack yelled to be heard over the pouring rain.

Alexia stepped between Wild and Jack and grabbed their hands. A hundred emotions boiled inside her. *Why must I go back? Why can't I stay and talk to Megan Staples?* She tightened her grip on the boys' hands.

"I hear it!" Jack shouted. "I hear my note! Get ready."

Alexia made her decision. She twisted her wrists and let go of both boys' hands, but their feet had already left the ground. Jack and Wild cried out. Wild lost his grip immediately, but Jack managed to hold on a few seconds, then … "No!" His fingers slipped from her wrist, and Alexia Dreager tumbled into a world of darkness.

Chapter 5

A TIMELY MEETING

The band of Awakened exploded through time as Alexia hurled from Jack like a stone from a sling. Jack gritted his teeth as he tightened his grip on Arthur's hand, but the circle was broken. Each member of the Awakened trailed behind Arthur, and every one of them was screaming.

Jack groaned as the others whipped about like a kite on a string. Wild and Andreal were the first to go. They launched into the darkness and were quickly followed by Mrs. Dumphry. All had vanished except for Arthur Greaves, who still clung to Jack's hand.

Alexia fell from the sky and crashed through a layer of ice, plunging beneath frigid waters. Her mind turned somersaults as she sank slowly downward. Unsure where she was or how she'd gotten there, she finally began kicking toward the surface, her cloak and clothes weighing her down.

She wanted to scream as she neared the surface. A layer of crystalline ice lay between her and the much-needed oxygen on the other side. She pounded at the frozen ceiling, raging at the moonlight taunting her from above. Her lungs burned, her movements slowed, and Alexia felt herself losing consciousness. *How could I be so stupid?* Her mind had cleared, and she knew it was her fault she was there. She'd made a terrible choice, letting go of Jack's hand. Her fingers slid along the ice, searching for any sign of weakness. *After everything I've been through, I'm going to drown, and it's all my fault!* Alexia stopped her searching and stared up at the full moon. It was beautiful. She sank into the darkness as something moved above the ice.

A cloaked figure began beating at the ice with a sword. *You're too late,* Alexia thought. *Whoever you are, you're too late.* She gasped for breath and inhaled. Her body jerked as frigid water spilled into her lungs.

Dirt and stalks of maize flew as Jack tumbled across the soft ground. When he finally skidded to a stop, he didn't move for a long time. He lay flat on his back somewhere in a maize field, gasping for breath and staring at the blue sky.

"Oh no!" he moaned. He sat up and pressed a palm hard against his forehead. "Oh no!" he said again.

"Are they … dead?" a voice said. Jack turned to see Arthur Greaves sitting on the ground.

"I let go," Arthur said. "I couldn't hold on. They were too heavy!" He pulled himself up to stand beside Jack.

Relief flooded Jack at the sight of his best friend. *But where are the others?* "Alexia!" he shouted. "Can you hear me? Mrs. Dumphry! Wild! Andreal! Where are you?"

Arthur let out a long breath. "The question is *when* are they? If they're alive, are they somewhere now, in our time, or are they back in the past?"

Jack hadn't thought of that.

"Is traveling through time like traveling on a steam train?" Arthur said. "If you step off the train before you arrive, are you somewhere between when you left and when you were going? And if so, where in the world would you be?" He began pacing. "Or does it even work like that? We were time traveling, after all. Alexia and the others could be somewhere a thousand years ago, or maybe even a thousand years in the future. Or maybe they're—"

"You're not helping!" Jack held up his hand. "I don't know the answer to any of it. I don't even know where or when we are! But we need to—"

"I would not move if I were you!" a gravelly voice called from somewhere nearby. "You are surrounded, and there is no chance of escape. Who are you? How did you come to be here?"

"I think I can summon the lightning," Arthur whispered. "I can feel it. It doesn't always come when I want, but I think it will now."

"You will answer my questions, or we will be forced to strike you down!" the voice called. "Are you dark servants, or do you follow the Author?"

"My name is Jack Staples, and I am one of the Children of Prophecy. Come out of hiding, and you will see the proof in my eyes. My friend's name is Arthur Greaves, and he is not someone you want to anger. Threaten us again, and you will regret it."

"What are you doing?" Arthur whispered. "We don't even know where they are or how many are out there."

"Whoever it is," Jack said with a smile, "they must be friends. We're in an Oasis. Can't you feel it?"

Arthur's jaw dropped. "You're right! I can't believe I didn't notice."

Jack inhaled. The air was impossibly fresh and invigorating to breathe. Besides that, they had landed hard, yet the ground had been incredibly soft. It was as if the earth had anticipated their arrival and cushioned itself. It was probably the only reason they hadn't broken any bones.

For a long moment, the voice was silent. Jack was beginning to wonder if anyone was still there, when he turned to see a very old man standing directly behind him. The man wore a brown cloak and carried a knobby walking staff. He had long gray hair and his thick beard went well below his waist. The last time Jack had see him was in the Council Chamber in the ruins of Agartha. He was a member of the Council of Seven.

"Honi?"

"It is good to see you again, Jack Staples, and you, too, Master Greaves. Welcome to the Great Oasis."

Alexia's eyes shot open. Something slammed into her chest again. She tried to breathe, but the icy water kept spilling out. She rolled onto her stomach and rose to her hands and knees, then finally gasped and filled her lungs with much-needed air.

"Whoa there, girl. You swallowed a lot of water," a man's voice said from just behind her. "You're going to be all right." A hand gripped Alexia's shoulder. "You just need to take it easy for a—"

She moved instinctively, twisting around to slam her fist into the man's gut. He let out a surprised grunt but didn't move back.

"That's one way to thank us for saving your life," he said.

Squatting beside the man was a boy. He looked to be close to her age and had a familiar face.

"Do I know you?" she croaked. The boy had dirty-blond hair, blue eyes, and a few whiskers on his chin and upper lip.

"I don't think so," the boy said. "I would have remembered if we'd met before."

"I'm sorry." Alexia coughed loudly, then turned to the man. Her throat was raw, and intense cold was seeping into her bones. Wherever she was, the world was blanketed in ice and snow. "I acted without thinking. Thank you for saving me. How did you find me?"

The man shrugged out of his cloak and placed it over Alexia's shivering frame. "It was Parker who saw you fall. He arrived first and pulled you out. And though I'd love to hear your story, I think we need to set a fire and get you warm first."

Alexia blinked. *It can't be.* She stood to get a better look at the man and the boy standing on the edge of a frozen lake. She knew who the boy reminded her of. He was the spitting image of her father ... *And he has Mother's eyes,* she thought sadly. *No ... he has his mother's eyes.*

The man's hair was raven black, just like hers, and she had his nose. "If he is Parker," she said tiredly, "then you must be Mr. Staples."

The man stiffened, placing a hand on the hilt of his sword. "How is it you know our names?"

"Because you are my father," Alexia said, "though I didn't find out until a few minutes ago." She was far too exhausted to understand what she was feeling. But seeing her father's face on Parker was all the proof she needed. Madeleine and Lloyd Dreager were not her birth parents; she was a Staples. "I also know that you have the Poet's Coffer. I know this because I helped give it to Parker just a few minutes ago."

Alexia dropped to the ice. All she wanted was to close her eyes and sleep. The cold saturated her bones, and her teeth began to chatter. Mr. Staples gathered her in his arms.

"You're going to be all right, my girl," he said. "I promise. Everything is going to be all right."

Alexia closed her eyes and fell into a fitful sleep as James Staples carried her into the woods.

Chapter 6

ONE MEMBER SHORT

Jack could barely make himself pay attention. He and Arthur had made it to the Great Oasis, but for all he knew, everyone else was either dead or scattered somewhere, or some-when, else. And he and Arthur weren't in the present but were still somewhere in the past, because the sun shone dazzlingly bright. The Assassin's Shadow had yet to swallow the sky.

Honi wasn't the only member of the Council of Seven at the Great Oasis. He'd brought Jack and Arthur to the Council Tent to meet a young woman with auburn hair and penetrating almond-colored eyes. Jack remembered seeing Sage in Agartha and thinking she was far too young to be on the Council. She couldn't be much older than he was.

"You have no idea if Alexia or the others are alive?" Sage asked for a second time.

"I don't know any more than I told you," Jack said. "I don't even know how I lost them. Maybe I wasn't concentrating enough or something."

"It's my fault," Arthur said. "I couldn't hold on. I wasn't strong enough."

"We are not assigning blame, Arthur," Sage said. "We are merely trying to learn what happened. I don't think your friends are dead. But there is nothing we can do about it now. The Last Battle will soon be upon us. We must continue to gather the newly Awakened and fight the Assassin with every bit of strength we have."

"We can't just leave them behind," Arthur said.

"And what would you have us do?" Honi stirred the fire with a stick. "We don't know where to look. Until we learn more, our friends must fend for themselves."

Arthur opened his mouth but shut it again. Jack also wanted to help his friends, but he knew Sage and Honi were right. What could they possibly do?

"Master Staples"—Honi gave his attention to Jack—"what do you know of Mrs. Dumphry's plans? How much has she told you?"

"We were to give the Poet's Coffer to Parker and then come back here. She didn't tell us anything else."

"It is good to see you again, Jack."

Jack turned to see a tall, older man he immediately recognized.

"King Edward!" He ran to the king. "What are you doing here?"

"After Miel's betrayal, the Council of Seven was one short. I was given the great honor of taking her seat." The king smiled warmly.

"I'd hoped our paths would cross again, but I hadn't thought it would be so soon."

Arthur watched the king with wide eyes. "You weren't joking, Jack. You do know the king!"

"Among the Awakened, I am no king." King Edward smiled. "I am merely Edward. When the palace fell, I gathered as many Awakened as I could and came here."

"I'm sorry, Your Majesty," Jack said. "I didn't know the palace had fallen."

"It fell the night you went through the World Portal. But in the war between darkness and light, palaces and titles are meaningless. I will miss my old home, but what matters most is in here." The king thumped his chest just above his heart. "So, where are Mrs. Dumphry and the others? And I can't wait to meet Alexia. I assume she came as well?"

Jack felt his throat tighten. "I'm sorry, but I don't know where they are. I don't even know if they're alive. I think I may have killed them all by accident."

"Ah, my dear boy"—the king chuckled—"the most powerful Shadow Souled on earth have been trying to kill Mrs. Dumphry for thousands of years. I doubt you were able to do it by accident. Yet I see there is a grim story here that needs telling." The king sighed as he sat beside Jack.

Jack nodded. "It all started when Arthur showed Mrs. Dumphry the Poet's Coffer." He could see the king was surprised, but he kept going. "We decided the best place to hide the coffer was in the past. That way the Assassin wouldn't be looking for it, because it would also still be in his throne room. And by the time he knew it was stolen, it would already be somewhere far away." Jack launched into the story for the second time since arriving at the Great Oasis.

Alexia opened her eyes to darkness. She didn't move as she listened to the world around her. Besides the wind and the hooting of an owl, she could hear the steady breathing of someone sleeping nearby. *How could I have been so stupid?* She berated herself. *I could have died. I could have killed the others!* She hadn't been thinking about the consequences of letting go of Jack's hand while traveling through time. Just before Alexia let go, she'd had a stray thought about Mr. Staples, wondering if she'd ever have the chance to meet her birth father. *Is that how I came to be here?*

She crawled from beneath the thick blankets, her eyes still adjusting to the dark. She saw the shadow of someone sitting nearby. *We're in a cave,* she realized. The ground was smooth rock and stars shone through the cavern mouth.

"Is there a reason you're trying to sneak up on me?"

Alexia tsked irritably. She'd been perfectly silent, yet still the boy had known she was there.

"How are you feeling?" Parker asked.

Alexia sighed, then walked over to sit on a rock opposite him. "Much better," she said. "Thank you for saving me."

"Of course," Parker said. "I'm just glad I got there in time."

For a long moment, Alexia and Parker stared into the darkness. The night sky was filled with so many stars, it was breathtaking. They were in a cavern on the side of a mountain.

Everything about this is strange, Alexia thought. She had a hundred questions for Parker but couldn't think where to begin.

"So what were they like?" he asked.

Alexia blinked. "What were who like?"

"My birth parents. I've often wondered about them, but Mother and Father never met them."

"So you knew?" Alexia asked. "That we were switched at birth?" She realized Parker must have almost as many questions as she did.

"They told me a little over a year ago. It's really strange, you know, because I love them. They are the best parents I could imagine. Yet I often find myself wondering what my birth parents were like."

"They were … they were the best parents in the world." Alexia's heart felt heavy. "They were strong and courageous, and all I ever wanted was to be like them."

"I feel the same way"—Parker nodded—"but it's nice to hear."

"You look like Father," she said without thinking. "Except you have Mother's eyes."

Parker smiled at that, but after a moment, the smile faded. "I'm sorry …" He stopped as if unsure how to continue. "I was only told they died a few months ago. But I felt terrible for you. I can't imagine losing a parent."

Alexia stiffened as tears sprang to her eyes. *He doesn't know!*

"Parker"—she reached out and grabbed his hand—"I don't know how to tell you this, but … your mother died a week after you and your father left. The Assassin came to Ballylesson, and she died saving me and Jack. I held her hand in the last moments."

Parker was silent. A long time passed as Alexia held his hand and waited. She knew what he was feeling and that there was nothing she could say.

"We should have been there," he said quietly. "We could have helped her. We could have done something!"

"Maybe," Alexia agreed. "But Jack went back in time and warned her. And even though she knew what was going to happen, she didn't run. She was very courageous."

Parker wiped his eyes. "It's going to destroy Father. We've been on the run since the day we left. We can't stay in the same place more than a day or two, or the enemy shows up. So we've had very little news. We know nothing of how the war is going or when the coffer will be needed. Mrs. Dumphry's note just said we must keep it safe at all costs."

"It's been really bad," Alexia said. "The Last Battle has begun and ..." She stopped and stared at the stars. If she were in the present, the Assassin's Shadow would have blotted out the sky. "I might be wrong actually," she said. "The Last Battle might not have begun just yet. I think maybe I'm still in the past somewhere."

"You may be in the past," Parker said, "but the rest of us are in the present."

Alexia nodded. Time travel was a dizzying subject.

"Will you tell me?" Parker asked. "About what's been happening?"

"Yes, but there is much to tell." Alexia leaned against the cavern wall. "A few days ago, we were in the City of Shadows, surrounded by a hundred thousand Shadow Souled."

"What were you doing there?" Parker said. "Was Jack with you?"

"Yes. Jack and Mrs. Dumphry, Aias, Andreal, Wild, and Arthur had come to rescue me from the Assassin."

"Wait, Arthur ... Greaves was with you?"

"Yes." Alexia grinned. "It was Arthur who saved us the first time around."

"He still had scales on his eyes last I saw him."

"Arthur saved us all. Elion said he might one day become the most powerful Awakened to walk the earth."

Parker let out a low whistle. "Now that's something I never would have believed."

"Me, either"—Alexia giggled—"especially with his annoying habit of sicking up all the time."

Parker chortled. "Now that sounds like the Arthur I know!"

"But my parents may still be there! What if they've been taken prisoner or are hurt or something?" Arthur stalked toward the entrance of the tent. "We have to go! We can't wait another minute."

"I am afraid Ballylesson is lost," Honi said. "There is nothing that can be done. Your hometown has become a stronghold of the Assassin and has been transformed into a place of monsters and nightmares."

Arthur looked to his friend. "We have to go find them, Jack. I don't care what he says." Arthur turned back to Honi. "Didn't you say there's a World Portal here?"

"The only humans left in Ballylesson are those who have chosen to follow the Assassin," King Edward said. "I'm sure your parents escaped before the evil grew too strong."

"I don't care. I have to go see. They're my parents!"

"But how did it happen?" Jack asked.

"Until today, we had no idea," Honi said. "We received reports over the past months that confirmed Ballylesson was changing, but nobody knew how or why. After hearing your story, I'd venture a guess. You said you stabbed the Assassin when you fought him on the street; is that correct?"

"I wouldn't say I fought him," Jack said, "but, yes, I did stab him."

"And what happened when you took the sword from his belly?"

Arthur knew his best friend didn't like talking about that day. Jack had fought the Assassin just minutes after his mother died.

Jack stabbed at the fire with a stick. "A dark wind exploded from the wound," he said, "though it only lasted a moment. And when his blood landed on the ground, it sizzled."

"Yes …" Honi scratched his chin through his thick beard. "It would be my guess that Ballylesson has been transmutated by the blood of the Assassin."

"What does that mean?" Arthur paced near the entry of the tent.

"Blood has power," Honi continued. "The streets and buildings of your hometown are covered in shadowed webs that grow thicker by the day. We know the poet's blood transforms whatever it touches, and I would guess the Assassin's blood has done the same. I'm sorry, boys, but your hometown has become a fortress of darkness that rivals the City of Shadows."

"We have to do something." Jack stood. "It's our home!"

"From what we understand, there is little we can do," Sage said. "The evil has spread too far."

"I have news from Mrs. Dumphry."

Arthur turned to see a young girl in a pretty dress standing just outside the tent. She nodded, then walked in and handed a rolled parchment to Sage.

"A pigeon arrived a few minutes ago." The girl looked to be two or three years younger than Arthur and had whimsical brown eyes and a mischievous smile.

"Thank you," Sage said as she unrolled the parchment. "This is my sister Aliyah. Aliyah, this is Jack and Arthur."

Aliyah curtsied.

"What does it say?" Jack demanded. "Is she alive?"

"Patience. I know as much as you." Sage thumbed the wax seal, then unfurled the scroll. As the scroll stretched out, Mrs. Dumphry's voice sounded inside the tent. Arthur shared an incredulous look with Jack.

There are three things you must always remember; three things that will guide you—forgiveness, mercy, and most of all, love. No matter the offense. No matter the pain that was caused. No matter how evil the action. If we do not offer mercy, if we are unable to forgive, we will never know love. You see, we do not forgive for the sake of our enemy; we forgive for the sake of our hearts.

In the midst of the Last Battle, you must remember these three truths. Choose love—always. Do not waste a moment worrying. Each moment spent in worry is a self-inflicted wound.

While traveling through time with young Jack Staples, the circle was broken, and I was sent through time. I have had the most wonderful adventure over these past years—

"Did she say 'years'?" Arthur asked.

Sage wore an astonished look as she unfurled the scroll a little more and Mrs. Dumphry's voice sprang up once again.

Though I send my greetings to all who are inside the Council Tent, I have instructions for Jack, Arthur, and Honi. So please listen carefully.

"How did she know we would be here?" Jack asked. Sage shook her head. Somehow, Mrs. Dumphry waited for their exchange before continuing.

It is imperative that we all meet in the Valley of Elah exactly two days after the Assassin's Shadow has swallowed the sky. The Assassin will be waiting for us there. Though the entire world will be locked in battle, our true fight is with the Father of Lies.

Many years ago I hid something of the utmost importance under the floorboards beneath my desk in the schoolhouse in Ballylesson. Young Jack Staples must take Honi and go to his hometown to retrieve it. Jack must lead the way and take no one else with him, or it will be sure death for everyone involved. And he must be careful, for I fear Ballylesson may have changed since last he was there.

Remember, fear is an imagined mountain. Believe it is real and climb the mountain if you wish, or you can step through it and lay hold of your destiny.

Sincerely,

Mrs. Dumphry

Sage shook her head at the abrupt ending. She unfurled the scroll a little more, then sighed. "Oh good, there's more." For one last time Mrs. Dumphry's voice sounded.

PS: Since I am far too busy at the moment, I offer my seat on the Council of Seven to young Arthur Greaves. He is strong and courageous, humble and wise. May the Author be with you in these final days.

"Wait!" Arthur blinked. "What did you say?"

Chapter 7

THE EYE OF THE LION

James Staples hadn't taken the news well. When he woke to take his turn on watch, Parker and Alexia had told him about the death of his wife. Mr. Staples hadn't said a word. He'd merely nodded and said they should get some sleep. That had been four nights ago, and he'd barely spoken since.

Alexia had decided to stay with Parker and Mr. Staples for a while because she wanted answers and she didn't know what else to do. She needed to find her mother and save her friends. But she had no idea how. *I'll go soon enough,* she thought, *but first I want to know a little more of what my birth father is really like.*

It was well past midnight when Alexia woke for her shift on watch. The enemy could sense the Poet's Coffer, so they had to be vigilant.

"I'll take watch now," Alexia said.

Mr. Staples didn't move. A few minutes passed, and Alexia began to wonder if he was sleeping.

"I'm sorry," he said. "I'm sorry I've been moping. Your news wasn't something I expected." He turned and met Alexia's eyes. "I didn't think anything could kill that woman. She was twice as fierce as any lion and infinitely more stubborn."

He has a kind face, she thought. "I spent a few days with her before … She was amazing. I've never met anyone like her."

"I have no doubt they were some of the best days of her life," Mr. Staples said. "Giving you up was the hardest thing we ever had to do. We love Parker." He glanced at his sleeping son. "I couldn't imagine life without him. But you were always in our thoughts."

"Why did you send me away?" Alexia asked. She didn't feel sad about it. She loved her parents very much. But she did want to know. "You sent me away, but you kept Jack. Why?"

"I wasn't there the night you were born," he said. "Until four days ago, I'd never laid eyes on my daughter. I wasn't even sure you were still alive. We heard about your parents and feared the worst."

Alexia was glad for the night. It hid the wetness on her cheeks.

Mr. Staples glanced at the sky. "Did Megan ever show you your star?"

"No," Alexia said. "What do you mean?"

"There." He pointed toward a circle of seven stars.

"You mean the *Lion's Eye?*" she asked.

"You know the constellations?"

"Yes, my father taught them to me." It felt a little funny talking to her birth father about her father. "The Lion's Eye." She pointed. "The Serpent's Tongue." She moved her arm again. "The Dreamer's Tree. Father and I spent many nights looking at the stars." Alexia squinted at the sky. "But the Lion's Eye looks brighter than I remember it. Is that possible?"

"It is indeed. In the very center of the eye, there are two stars. Most people think there is only one because they are so close together. But if you look closely, you'll see it."

Alexia nodded. She'd never noticed the second star before, but now she could see it.

"The center of the Lion's Eye was dark; it was just a ring of seven stars. At the moment of your birth, your star was born, and it blazed so bright, it outshone the moon." He shook his head wonderingly. "I knew you'd been born, and I was desperate to get back to Ballylesson to meet you. As I journeyed home, the star faded. And by the time I returned, it was gone."

"What do you mean it was gone? It's right there." Alexia's eyes strayed to the star.

"The star was a sign of your coming. The Child of Prophecy had been born, and anyone who knew the signs could see it. But I was with Mrs. Dumphry on a mission of great importance. We'd traveled to the Forbidden Garden to meet with Time. When we saw the star, we were still weeks from home. I knew Megan was the Chosen One, but when your star faded, my heart was gripped with fear. What did it mean? Had you really been born? Had something terrible happened?"

Alexia was mesmerized. Hearing about the night of her birth, learning that a star was born to herald her coming—there was something magical about it.

"When I arrived at the house, I was relieved to find that everything seemed normal. I held Parker in my arms, and when Mrs. Dumphry and I looked into his eyes, it was obvious he was not the Child of Prophecy. It was only after Mrs. Dumphry left that Megan told me what happened."

Mr. Staples pulled a chain from around his neck. At the end of the chain was a small black stone streaked with blue veins. "Do you know what this is?" He held it up to the moonlight. The veins flickered as the stone caught the light.

Alexia nodded. "It's a Memory Stone. I've used them twice before."

"This was Megan's. She gave it to me the morning Parker and I left with the Poet's Coffer. It contains her favorite memories and has made the days away more bearable." Pain passed over him again. "I'm sorry," he said. "It still doesn't feel real."

Alexia waited. After a moment he shook his head and handed her the stone. "If you want to see what truly happened on the night you were born, hold the stone and think on the memory."

Alexia's hands shook as her fingers closed around the small stone. Mr. Staples offered a warm smile and nodded encouragingly. She took a deep breath and formed the thought in her mind as the world shifted.

Alexia was in Jack's bedroom back in Ballylesson. Megan Staples lay on a small bed. She was soaked in sweat and screaming as Elion knelt beside her. The Sephari's eyes sparkled like diamonds as she patted Megan's forehead with a wet towel.

"You're nearly there," Elion said. "Once more, and your baby will be here."

Megan squeezed Elion's hand as she screamed again and gasped. Alexia stood by her side, watching. It was surreal, being there at the moment of her birth. A moment later, Elion lifted the baby, cradling it in a thick blanket.

"It's a girl," she said. "And there is no doubt. She is the Child of Prophecy." White light exploded through the window as Alexia's star was birthed; neither Elion nor Megan seemed to notice.

Elion's eyes turned sunset orange as she handed the baby to Megan.

"I have entered this memory a thousand times."

Alexia turned to see Mr. Staples. She hadn't realized he'd come with her. All of his attention was given to his wife and newborn daughter. "It is my greatest regret that I wasn't there the night you were born. I only wanted to hold you." Tears shone in his eyes.

Megan Staples held baby Alexia close. Elion sat beside her and smiled happily.

"But why? Why was I taken away?" Alexia asked.

Mr. Staples waved his hand, and the world shifted once again. They were in the same room, but Megan was standing by the window cradling baby Alexia. "This is only a few hours later," he said.

Baby Alexia had a full head of raven-black hair and a small dimple in her cheek.

"Alexia," Megan said through teary eyes. "Her name is Alexia Staples."

"It is a beautiful name," Elion said. The Sephari had donned her Atherial Cloak. She was almost impossible to see.

A look of anguish crossed Megan's face. "It's not fair. She's less than a day old!" she said. "She needs her mother! I can't give my daughter away before her father has a chance to meet her." Megan sighed. "How can you ask this of me, Elion?"

"And you think you can keep her safe from what's coming? You think you can stop him?"

For a moment Megan looked as if she was going to argue; then she began to cry. "But this is my child. She is mine!"

"This is the Child of Prophecy, and you know as well as I do that he is coming. If I don't take her now, all will be lost." She turned her gaze to the cloudless sky. "We are not the only ones who can read the stars."

Alexia stood beside Megan and Elion, and all three women looked up at the sky. At the center of the Lion's Eye was a mammoth star that was indeed brighter than the moon. Though it should not have been possible, the star looked to be directly above the Stapleses' house.

"Mother, what's going on?"

Elion spun as Megan shielded baby Alexia with her body.

In less than a heartbeat, Elion had drawn her sword as colored mist rose from the floorboards. "Who are you, boy?" she demanded. "Speak now or die!"

"What?" Alexia breathed. Jack Staples was standing in the doorway.

Elion's eyes blazed. Jack stood with his mouth agape, staring.

"Mother, it's me, Jack! What's going on?"

"Look at his eyes!" Elion stepped closer.

"What do you mean?" Megan took a cautious step forward.

"Come here, boy." Elion lowered her sword and offered Jack her hand. He took it, looking as if he were trying to wake from a bad dream.

Jack must have time traveled here, Alexia thought. *But not on purpose, or he wouldn't look so confused.* Megan stepped closer, gazing into Jack's eyes. "What does it mean?" she whispered. And then an impossibly bright light exploded through the room. Jack disappeared in a burst of wind.

For a long moment, neither Megan nor Elion spoke. Alexia and Mr. Staples also stood silent, watching the memory.

"This changes everything," Elion whispered.

"I don't … I don't understand," Megan said. "He called me 'Mother'!"

"The only explanation is that you are his mother. And by his eyes it is clear. He is the Child of Prophecy."

"What?" Megan sat in the rocking chair next to the window. "Look at her eyes, Elion! Alexia was born without scales."

Elion's eyes became a swirl of color. "It does make sense," she said. She gazed toward the sky once again as a small smile crept onto her lips. "Look at Alexia's star."

Megan stood and looked up. The impossibly bright star at the center of the Lion's Eye was already fading.

"There are two children," Elion said excitedly. "Male and female, brother and sister. I have told you before that you humans are unlike anything the Author has created. In all the worlds, of all the creatures, beasts and beings, you are special. You are like the Author himself. He has woven himself into your very souls, and his blood runs in your veins."

Elion lovingly stroked baby Alexia's cheek. "Yet the Author is neither male nor female." She began to laugh. "I can't believe we didn't see it before! Two children—it's the only thing that makes sense! If the Child of Prophecy has any chance of destroying the Assassin, the child must fully represent the Author, male and female!"

Alexia's mind turned somersaults as she listened.

"You must tell no one except James," Elion said. "There are those who would betray this information to the Assassin. We must keep Alexia a secret for as long as we can." Elion looked at the moon again. "My guess is her star will fade until your son is born. One child is simply not strong enough to stand against the coming darkness. But when Jack is born, his star will reflect hers, and together their light will grow."

Elion placed a hand on Megan's shoulder. "I know what I am asking of you is impossible, but if you keep her, Alexia will be in grave danger. If we can hide her away, the world will never know the first Child of Prophecy has been born. Yes, they will still come, but they will think they misread the stars. Only when I've made the switch will she be safe."

Alexia blinked as the world shifted again.

Alexia was back on the mountainside with Mr. Staples. For a long moment, she didn't speak. She held tight to the stone and tried to understand. "But why wasn't Jack sent away?"

"When Jack was born, his star also burned brighter than the moon. And within hours it, too, faded. Then your star and Jack's began to reflect each other, each star's light feeding the other. And they will continue to grow brighter the closer you come to fulfilling your destiny."

Mr. Staples stood and scanned the valley below. "The Child of Prophecy had come," he continued, "and there was no hiding it. But this time we were ready. We knew Jack's star would point toward his birthplace. So we placed Blinding Stones around Ballylesson and took other precautions. Ballylesson was as safe a place as any to—"

Mr. Staples stiffened, looking at the valley below. "There." He pointed toward a large grouping of trees at the foot of the valley.

At first Alexia didn't see anything, but after a moment, she realized the trees were … moving! *What?* At least thirty large trees were gliding up the canyon. They were moving quickly and would top the rise within minutes.

"We need to leave, now," Mr. Staples said. "Wake Parker and gather your things."

Alexia didn't waste time with questions. Parker's eyes shot open the moment she knelt beside him. "We need to go," she whispered. "The trees are"—she wasn't sure how to say it—"coming."

Parker nodded and began gathering his things. Mr. Staples grabbed them from Parker, then placed a hand on his shoulder. "Be safe," he said. "We'll see you at the top of the rise." He turned to Alexia. "Follow me."

"We're leaving him here?"

"Trust me," Parker said. "You don't want to be anywhere near what's about to happen."

"There's no time to explain," Mr. Staples said. He turned and ran into the darkness. Alexia waited only a moment. Parker offered a roguish grin that reminded her of Wild. *Boys,* she thought irritably, then rolled her eyes and followed Mr. Staples.

They sprinted up the icy slope, and by the time they reached the top, they were sweating despite the snow. He stopped and turned his attention back down the slope. Alexia found Parker quickly. He stood atop a large boulder, bathed in moonlight.

"Why did we leave him?"

"Just because there is a battle to fight doesn't mean you are meant to fight it. Parker's Soulprint is what is needed here."

The trees were close now. She squinted, wishing for more light. Besides the obvious, there was something different about these trees. The branches stretched farther than should have been possible, and long, spindly vines whipped ahead to strike into the ground and propel them forward.

Alexia watched in horror as the enormous things surrounded Parker. Vines wrapped his body, lifting him into the air. He didn't even try to fight back. *He's going to be torn to pieces.* "We have to do something!"

"Just wait." Mr. Staples's voice was tight. "All we can do now is wait."

The vines pulled Parker inward as the trees swallowed him up. Alexia balled her fists, itching to run down and help. She was at home in the trees. Surely she could do something. She glanced at Mr. Staples and saw both fear and pride in his eyes.

The trees continued forward at a rapid pace. Alexia searched behind, looking for any sign of Parker, but he was gone. "No," she whispered. Suddenly a piercing ... *something* erupted from deep within the trees. It was a terrifying keening that made Alexia want to claw at her ears. The trees thrashed about as something rippled through the length and breadth of their trunks. They lurched to a stop as their limbs dried up, turning brittle. The vines and leaves withered and dropped to the ground.

Alexia pressed her palms hard against her ears in an unsuccessful attempt to block out the sound. Thick trunks crumbled. The sounds faded into nothing, and the world became eerily silent.

Standing in the center of the destruction was Parker. His clothes were torn and he was covered in dead vines, but other than that, he seemed perfectly fine.

"What did he do?"

"I'm not sure," Mr. Staples said. "And neither is he. I've seen a single tree take down a hundred Awakened before it was finally destroyed. Parker's Soulprint allows him to fight back." Mr. Staples breathed a sigh of relief. "In truth, this is the first time Parker has fought more than three at once. His Soulprint has grown strong this past year."

"There were a least thirty of them! If he's only ever fought three, how did you know he could win now?"

"Because he had to. Each one of us has been born with a very special and very specific purpose. The Author has given each of us abilities that only we can express. Not everyone has powers like you or Parker or myself. For some, the Soulprint is an extra helping of wisdom or kindness. But whatever it is, there will be a time in everyone's life when only he or she can do what needs to be done. Tonight was at least one of the reasons Parker was born. This is one of his many gifts. You and I could have stayed and fought, but we'd most likely have died without ever slowing the trees."

Parker was still ripping dead vines from his body when he reached the top of the rise. When he saw Alexia, he grinned. "Impressed?"

"Yes. Very," she said.

Mr. Staples patted Parker on the back. "You did well." He scanned the canyon. "I'm afraid the Shadow Souled have discovered our trail once again. We need to go before something worse comes."

Arthur realized his mouth was hanging open. "You can't be serious!" he gasped. "This must be some kind of bad joke." He stood in the Council Tent alongside Honi, King Edward, and Sage. "I don't even turn twelve till next month!" He wished Jack were there to back him up, but his best friend had been asked to wait outside.

"It is not age that brings wisdom," Honi replied, "but experience and humility. And though you are young, you are rich in both. This is no joke, Master Greaves; Mrs. Dumphry would not have passed her seat to you unless she was absolutely certain. She is wiser than anyone on earth, and it is her right to give away her seat."

"Arthur, I'm only thirteen," Sage said. "Do you think I should not be a member of the Council?"

"Of course not! But you're wise and beautiful and obviously know a lot about a lot of things, and I bet you're a proper hero. But I'm just a boy from Ballylesson. Surely there must be others you could ask!"

"Of course there are," King Edward said. "But we are asking you."

"There's so much I don't know!"

"Although your scales fell off less than a year ago, you are no child," Honi said. "Is it true you once tackled a Shadule just to save your friend? And was it you who rescued Mrs. Dumphry and the others from the arena in the City of Shadows? Oh, and there was something else ..." Honi tapped his temple with his finger. "Am I remembering incorrectly that it was you who stole the Poet's Coffer?"

"Well, yes," Arthur said. "But I didn't do any of that stuff because I was brave. I just did what had to be done, that's all."

King Edward burst out laughing as Sage smiled.

"Most of all, you deserve this position precisely because you don't want it," Honi said. "It is character that unearths greatness, not power. Everything pales in the light of character."

He was sure they were wrong. He knew he would make a terrible Council member. Now that he thought about it, he didn't even know what a Council member did, other than sit around in Council meetings. But there was no point in arguing further.

"Will you accept the offer? Will you join us on the Council of Seven?" King Edward asked.

Arthur nodded. Honi smiled as King Edward clapped his hands and Sage grinned.

"It will be good to have your wisdom as we prepare the Awakened for the Last Battle. Please," Sage said, "take your seat. There are a great many things we must discuss. But first let us speak of battle strategies."

As he sat down, Arthur Greaves wanted to cry.

Chapter 8

A BAD DAY INDEED

Alexia, Parker, and Mr. Staples had barely slept since the night the trees attacked. They'd been unable to stay more than a few hours ahead of the pursuing Shadow Souled.

"Do you think they know you have the Poet's Coffer?" Alexia asked as they trudged across a wide valley. The deep snow made it slow going even with the snowshoes Mr. Staples had fashioned for them.

Parker shared a look with his father. "The thing is," Parker said quietly, "we don't have it."

Alexia stopped. "What do you mean you don't have it? Isn't that what you've been doing out here, trying to keep it safe?"

"Yes," Mr. Staples agreed. "But you must understand, the Poet's Coffer doesn't just carry his most prized possessions, but it also carries his presence. To the eyes of the Shadow Souled, the coffer is like a bonfire on a hill in the dark of night." He stopped and turned to Alexia. "Mrs. Dumphry's plan was brilliant. The Shadow Souled don't suspect we have it, or they would have sent legions after us. They have no idea we have it because the coffer is still safe in the Assassin's throne room. We are in the past, and Arthur has yet to steal it from the City of Shadows."

"But that's exactly the reason you were meant to keep it safe," Alexia said. "Where is it now?"

"We left it behind," Parker said. "A few nights before I found you, we were trapped by a hundred Shadow Souled and didn't think we'd live to see another day. So we buried it beneath fifty Blinding Stones and kept running. But because Father carried the coffer for so long, the poet's presence still rests on him."

"We did what we had to do," Mr. Staples said. "We'd hoped to lose them and circle back to collect it later, but each time we think we're safely away, they find us again."

"And how do you know they don't have it already?" Alexia asked. "Maybe they found it."

"I don't think so." Mr. Staples pulled his cloak tight as the wind picked up. "The stones agreed to blind the eyes of evil. They understood the importance of the coffer."

Alexia stopped. "What do you mean they 'agreed'? They're stones, aren't they?"

"And the trees that attacked were 'just trees,' weren't they?" Parker swallowed his grin when he saw the dangerous look in Alexia's eyes.

"Blinding Stones are just stones that have awakened," Mr. Staples said. "They've agreed to join the Author and fight the Assassin. Some become Blinding Stones; others, Healing Stones or Memory Stones or all sorts of things. We found as many awakened stones as we could and asked if they'd help."

"And they … talked to you?"

"No." Mr. Staples chuckled. "The stones can't talk. We know they agreed because they did as we asked. Once the coffer was buried beneath them, they embraced their higher purpose and became Blinding Stones."

Alexia didn't know why this surprised her. It seemed that every day she was learning another reason why the world was far more fantastical than she'd imagined.

"My new plan is to lead these Shadow Souled to the Great Oasis you told us about," Mr. Staples said. "Once we arrive, we can have the Awakened help us destroy them. If the Author wills it, we will return with an army to retrieve the coffer."

Alexia thought for a moment. "I need to leave you," she said sadly.

"I don't think that's a good idea," Mr. Staples said. "You are even more important than the coffer; we need to keep you safe."

"If the Assassin's servants can feel the coffer on you, doesn't it make sense that I should stay as far from you as possible?" Alexia shook her head. "Besides, I'm not asking your permission; I'm telling you my decision. I've learned my mother might still be alive. I don't know where she is, but I plan to find her. And after I've found her, I have some friends who need my help. Once these things are done, I will find the Awakened and do whatever is needed."

Parker and Mr. Staples shared a look, but neither said a word.

"What?" Alexia asked. "What aren't you telling me?"

"She asked, Father. We have to tell her."

"I know." Mr. Staples sighed, then gave Parker a sharp nod.

Parker fished inside his jacket and pulled out a crumpled letter. "This is the letter I found in my pocket the morning after the circus fire. With the coffer." Parker handed it to Alexia. "The front of it says to leave right away and to keep the coffer safe at all costs, but read what the back says."

Alexia took the letter, then turned it over and read aloud.

In your travels, you may meet a girl who claims to be from both the past and the future. If so, you must keep her safe at all costs. And if she ever asks about her adopted mother, you must allow her to read this note.

Alexia glanced at Parker. "How could she possibly have known I would be here?"

Parker shook his head. Alexia continued reading.

Child, forgive me for not telling you the news before now. But I have recently learned your mother is alive and has been the Assassin's captive for many years. She is being held in the throne room in the City of Shadows. To try and rescue her will most likely lead to your death, but I understand you must try.

Remember, you don't utilize your Soulprint through control; you activate it by surrendering to it. It is not something you do but something you allow to be done through you.

Sincerely,

Mrs. Dumphry

Alexia drew in a sharp breath. Could it be true? She crumpled the letter in her fist. *I was in the throne room every night for weeks! How could Mother possibly have been there?* "I'm leaving." Alexia turned toward the south and took a step.

"It will take weeks to reach the City of Shadows, and even if you do, you'll be on your own." Mr. Staples placed a hand on her shoulder. "Please, you must not do this. Come with us to the Great Oasis, and we'll get help. Once the coffer is safely retrieved, I'll go with you myself."

"Thank you." Alexia wiped away tears. "I'm very glad to have met you both. You are a good man, Mr. Staples, and I do hope we'll meet again. But I must go."

Mr. Staples wrapped Alexia in a hug. "If there were any other way, I'd go with you," he whispered.

"I know," Alexia said as she hugged him back.

The following weeks were dreadful for Alexia. She barely stopped to sleep or eat for fear she'd be too late to rescue her mother. Whenever she had managed sleep, it had been in the tops of the dead trees or high up in the cleft of a large boulder. Each time she closed her eyes, her dreams were haunted with images of the Assassin torturing her mother. Alexia had seen blessedly few Shadow Souled on her journey, and none had seen her, not even the creature she'd knocked out so she could steal its cloak.

Her feet crunched on charred ground as she approached the City of Shadows; only desolation remained. The enormous gilded gate stood open; not a soul could be seen.

Standing bold against the yellow sky at the far corner of the city was the colossal arena. The cries of thousands of dark servants gathered there echoed through the empty streets, and the sky above the coliseum was filled with winged monsters.

Alexia pulled back the hood of her stolen black-and-silver cloak. She thought she'd need it to sneak inside, but she'd arrived at the perfect time. She took a deep breath and stepped forward.

"Do you mind if I join you?" The voice was directly behind her. She spun and slammed her fist into her attacker's midriff. Just as she was about to follow with a knee to the face, she stopped.

"Parker? What are you doing here?"

"It's good to see you, too," he groaned. "You really need to stop hitting people for no reason."

"You really need to stop sneaking up on people!"

"I've been trying to catch up to you ever since you left, but you've been moving at an impossible pace."

"But why? Why did you follow? And where is your father?"

"After you left, we agreed that one of us should help you free your mother. And Father still carries the poet's presence. So it had to be me."

Alexia felt as if she were going to cry. She balled her fists, trying to keep hold of her emotions.

"You're not going to try and hit me again, are you?" Parker raised his hands.

She moved without thinking and wrapped her arms around him. "I'm so glad you came," she whispered. "I didn't want to go in there by myself."

Parker hugged her close. "I don't blame you. I can barely look at it without shivering."

Alexia wiped a tear from her eye. The City of Shadows was indeed a place of nightmares. Detached shadows slithered at the corners of her vision, and though the streets were empty, she still had the feeling of being watched.

"What's your plan?" Parker scanned the streets. "And where is everyone?" His eyes drifted to the arena.

"We don't have much time," Alexia said. "Every dark servant in the city has gathered in the arena to watch me bow before the Assassin—I mean, the me from the past. In just a little while, I'm going to decide not to bow … and that's when the slaughter begins."

"Should we go to the palace now? If your mother is there, wouldn't it be best—"

"No, my friends have been held prisoner here for years. And it was my fault they were captured. I will escape this city in a few hours, but my friends and many more Awakened will be recaptured. I'm not leaving here until we save every last prisoner."

Parker let out a low whistle. "I don't know if we can do it, but I'm with you."

Alexia hadn't expected him to agree. In truth, she'd hoped he'd try and talk her out of it. It was ridiculous. How could they possibly save everyone? She knew what was about to happen. A hundred thousand Shadow Souled were going to swarm over the Awakened, and only a handful would escape.

"We'll need to break into the prison and free my gang first," she said. "They can help us free Mother, and then we can decide how to get the rest of them out."

"Don't people usually break out of prisons?" Parker said with a tight smile.

"Not today," Alexia said.

"They want you to come in now. And you're not going to believe who's waiting inside!" Arthur said.

Jack turned. "So did you accept?" he asked. "Have you become a member of the Council of Seven?"

Arthur nodded, though he suddenly looked as if he'd eaten a rotten apple. "I think they just made the biggest mistake in the world."

Jack punched Arthur's shoulder. "You are the most courageous person I know. You can do this!"

Arthur blushed. "We'd better get back in. You've got a surprise ... but I'll let you see for yourself."

When they stepped inside, Jack gasped. "Father!" James Staples stood inside the tent, talking quietly with Honi, King Edward, and Sage.

"Jack!" As his father turned, a burst of light and wind exploded inside the tent, and something slammed into Jack's chest, knocking him to the ground.

Jack looked up to see an Odius hulking above him. The beast was in the shape of a sleek jaguar and the ring of eyes that wrapped around its head were focused on him. The metallic creature shook its head as if dazed, and for a moment nobody moved. *It's the Odius from the circus!*

The Odius roared as a wall of liquid electricity slammed into it, wrapping it like a glove, holding it in midair. Jack scrambled away as the creature contorted into the shape of a seven-headed snake, each head straining against its prison of light.

"I can't hold it much longer!" Arthur screamed. He was standing on his toes, swaying, with both arms raised. The light exploded from the seven-headed snake and fastened itself around Arthur, imprisoning him with his own Soulprint. *An Odius can read a Soulprint and imitate it,* Mrs. Dumphry had told them.

Jack's father unsheathed his sword and became transparent as he stepped through the Odius. All seven heads struck at him but couldn't touch him. His father solidified again and struck, but his sword ricocheted off the monster's rippling skin.

Honi sent a spinning whirlwind at the creature as Sage leaped over it like a cat and struck out with a clawed hand. King Edward darted, then slammed a fist into the monster, sending it flying back through the tent, tumbling across the ground.

When it rose again, the Odius was a mammoth spider. Silvery webs shot from the spinnerets on its abdomen and wrapped around Jack's feet, dragging him screaming across the ground. A wall of liquid light wrapped around Jack's father and the king. Sage leaped at it again, but the Odius became momentarily transparent. It was now using all of their Soulprints.

"I will consume your soul," the spider wheezed as it pulled Jack inexorably closer. Jack clawed at the ground but couldn't find anything to grab.

Suddenly the ground beneath the Odius gave way. The spider shrieked and sank downward. A nearby oak tree flowed across the ground and slammed a thick branch into the beast even as vines shot from the earth to wrap tightly around it.

The silvery webbing dissipated, and Jack scrambled back. The Odius shrieked and broke free from the vines, but more trees surrounded it as a hundred Clear Eyes arrived. A wolf leaped at the Odius as an eagle swept down, tearing into the rippling skin with its razor talons. The Odius fought free only to fall into another sinkhole. It battled its way out again, but before it could do anything, a bear leaped onto its back and pinned it to the ground.

Vines sprang up, binding it to the ground as the trees moved in again. Every eye ringing the gurgling Odius's head was wide in terror as the creature was pulled deep into the earth. The shields of light imprisoning the Awakened evaporated, and for a long moment, nobody moved.

The ground solidified as grass and flowers sprang up to erase any sign that the Odius had ever been there. One by one, the Clear Eyes turned into the forest.

Jack's father pulled him to his feet and wrapped him in a hug. "I don't know what just happened, but it's good to see you, Son. I'm so glad you're safe."

Jack hugged his father fiercely.

"It shouldn't have been possible for a Shadow Souled to enter an Oasis, let alone appear in our midst without warning," Honi said.

Jack released his father, then turned to Honi. "I think I brought it here. When it arrived, it was in the same form as when it tried to kill me at the circus. But just before it attacked the younger me, it disappeared in a burst of light ..." He looked at his father. "I was thinking about you in that moment. I thought I'd never get to see you again. Maybe that's why it arrived here, when we were both together."

"That is a very powerful Soulprint indeed, young Jack," King Edward said. "To be able to send your enemy through time and space. Powerful and dangerous. I've seen an Odius defeat hundreds of Awakened in a matter of minutes. It was the Author's favor that you sent it to an Oasis."

"Next time you decide to do such a thing," Honi said with a half smile, "I'd think long and hard about where and when you send your enemy." He turned to Jack's father. "You and Jack need some time to catch up, but sit with us awhile. We'd love to hear about your journey, and I for one am itching to see the Poet's Coffer."

"I have bad news about the coffer. I've not had it for almost six weeks now. As far as I know, it is still safely hidden away. But we'll need to leave immediately if we are to retrieve it."

"Father, is Parker with you?" Jack asked.

"Parker left me almost a month ago. He went to help Alexia rescue her mother."

"Alexia was with you?" Jack and Arthur asked in unison.

"She's all right, then? How did you find her?" Jack grabbed his father's arm excitedly.

"She dropped from the sky like a shooting star into a frozen lake. Parker arrived just in time to save her." Jack's father wrapped an arm around Arthur as he spoke. "It's good to see you, Arthur. Alexia told me of your Soulprint, but it's another thing entirely to see you work it. Not one in a thousand Awakened would have been strong enough to stop an Odius like you just did."

Arthur grinned. "Do you know anything of my parents?" he asked. "Do you know where they are or if … or if they are …"

Jack knew what his friend was trying to say: *Do you know if my parents are alive?*

"I'm sorry, my boy, but the only news I've received this past year came from Alexia." He met Jack's eyes. "She told me about your mother," he said. "I'm sorry I wasn't there. I know it was terrible."

"It wasn't your fault." Jack sighed. "It was the Assassin's. I know that now. It wasn't my fault either. But I'm going to finish him, Father."

Chapter 9

EVERY LAST ONE

"I still don't understand why you can't come with me," Jack said. "We've only had a few hours together!"

"If there were any other way, I would," his father said. "But your task cannot wait, and neither can mine. Besides, Mrs. Dumphry's letter made it clear that only Honi was to go with you. And I am the only one who knows where to find the coffer. But the moment the coffer is back in the hands of the Awakened, I will find you no matter where you are. And if the Author wills it, I will fight by your side in the Last Battle."

James Staples wrapped his son in a hug, and Jack melted into his arms. "I don't know if I can lead," Jack whispered.

"You'll do well. You have always been a leader, Jack. I believe in you. Just listen to your heart. You must learn to recognize the Author's voice. It is the whisper of a whisper, and he is always speaking." His father leaned back and looked him in the eye. "I love you, Son."

"I love you, too, Father."

Without another word, Jack's father stepped into the spinning World Portal.

Jack stood and watched with a heavy heart. It wasn't fair.

"He's right, you know," Arthur said. "You have always been a leader. You saved me from Jonty Dobson in the schoolyard before you even knew who I was."

Jack smiled. "And we both know how well that turned out." Jonty Dobson had thrown the boys into a mud puddle. "I wish we could stay together."

"I'd give anything to go back to Ballylesson," Arthur replied, "even if it has changed. But, Jack, if my parents are still there, you have to promise me you won't leave them behind."

"Of course," Jack said, "I promise."

Arthur smiled. "I'll see you soon," he whispered.

"You be careful," Jack said. "Just because you're on the Council doesn't make you invincible. And don't go getting a big head about it."

Arthur laughed as he turned and stepped into the spinning rings of the World Portal with Jack's father and the others. Jack met his father's eyes as the rings filled with thick, green liquid. When it reached the top of the rings, the small band of Awakened disappeared in a flash of light.

For a long moment, Jack didn't move. He knew Honi was waiting. He knew he should turn around and say something. But he wanted one final moment to be a kid. Until now he'd relied on Mrs. Dumphry to tell him where to go and what to do. It had been hard, but it was nothing compared to what he was feeling now. He took a deep breath.

"All right, then, I guess it's time we leave as well."

Honi smiled encouragingly. "I will follow your lead."

Jack placed his hands on the steel rings. They felt silky beneath his fingers. "Ballylesson," he said. The rings began to spin, and Jack Staples stepped inside.

Alexia and Parker sprinted into the darkened corridors of the arena as the sky began to fall. Alexia's heart sank. The Alexia from the past was sprinting away from Korah and the Assassin. Alexia watched herself run straight at the hulking Drogule that held her friends captive with a cable of electrified light.

She and Parker stood behind a pillar as dark servants rushed past them into the arena. The Alexia from the past reached the Drogule and dove into the cable of light, freeing Mrs. Dumphry and the others. Andreal roared and took three running steps, crashing into the monster as Wild pulled Alexia to her feet. The small band of Awakened quickly formed a circle, standing back to back. A split second before the Shadow Souled collided with them, a shield of blue light formed around them.

Monsters from the sky and the arena crashed into the shield. Alexia watched as the dark servants continued pushing in, crawling over each other in an attempt to kill the Awakened, but they were far too bloodthirsty to see what was happening. The sky emptied, and the mountain of dark flesh grew wider and higher.

"I can't believe anyone survived that." Parker stood with his mouth agape. On either side of the pillar, the last stragglers of the Shadow Souled rushed in.

Before Alexia could answer, a burst of dusty wind exploded from the mountain of flesh. Suddenly most of the dark servants stopped moving. Alexia still didn't know how she'd done it, but she was certain the Alexia from the past had knocked the beasts unconscious.

"We should go," she said. Looking at it now, she agreed with Parker. She'd lived through it and still had no idea how any of them had survived. She turned to walk back into the corridor, but Parker placed a hand on her shoulder.

"Is that … Arthur?"

Alexia turned to see Arthur Greaves entering the arena. He moved gracefully, spinning round and kicking his feet in an odd-looking dance. Where he moved, a towering wedge of liquid light moved with him. The wedge slid into the mountain of flesh to shove it aside.

"Yes," Alexia said, "we need to get below before things get worse."

"It gets worse?" Parker squeaked. "Where are we going?"

"We're going to face our fears," Alexia said grimly.

Arthur exited the emerald Sea of Worlds and tumbled across the muddy ground. Just behind him came Sage, Aliyah, King Edward, and Mr. Staples. All he could think about was Jack. *What if he needs me and I'm not there?*

"He's going to be all right," Mr. Staples said as he stood and wiped his muddy hands on his coat. "I'm worried about him too, but Jack's going to be fine. Now let's find the coffer and get it back to the … Oh no."

Arthur turned and wanted to scream. They stood at the edge of … "What is it?"

"It's a Quagmire," Mr. Staples said. "It must have formed around the coffer."

Arthur felt sick to his stomach. The only thing he knew about Quagmires was that they were the opposite of the Oases. They were the gathering places for every form of evil; Mrs. Dumphry said that to enter one would be a quick and brutal death.

"Does that mean the Assassin has the coffer?" Sage asked.

"No." Mr. Staples shook his head. "I doubt he knows it's there. There were fifty Blinding Stones guarding it. But his servants must still be able to feel it even if they don't know what it is. I'd bet the Quagmire began forming within hours of our hiding it away."

"So what now?" Arthur asked. "We can't go in there."

All five Awakened stood side by side staring at the wall of corruption. The border was a tangle of thorny vines and sickly looking bushes, and it was expanding even as they watched.

"I'm afraid there's no other choice," Mr. Staples said. "To enter this Quagmire will most likely be the death of us all. But to lose the Poet's Coffer will be the death of the world." He placed his hands on Arthur's and Sage's shoulders. "I know it's much to ask, but I'll ask it anyway. Will you join me in retrieving the Poet's Coffer? There is no shame in staying back."

"I'm with you," Arthur said quickly. He wanted to get the words out before he had a chance to think them through.

"I will be honored to join you in such a worthy task," King Edward said.

"I will go," Sage said.

"As will I," Aliyah added.

"Good! When we enter, we must do so at an all-out run. No matter what happens, we cannot slow. If we stop moving forward, we'll become trapped." Mr. Staples pointed toward a mountain of black stone that rose in the center of the Quagmire. "The Poet's Coffer is there, at the base of the mountain. When we arrive, you will have to guard my back as I unbury it."

Arthur felt his stomach sink a little farther. The base of the mountain was at least an hour's run from the ever-expanding border. Dense and corrupted jungle filled the space between. He'd been thinking they'd have to run a few minutes at most.

Mr. Staples unsheathed his sword as King Edward's skin transformed to thickened leather. Arthur reached out for his Soulprint and sighed in relief as he felt the electricity on his skin. Aliyah bowed her head, and thin, white wings extended from her back.

"What?" she said as she raised her bow and nocked an arrow. "You've never seen a girl with wings before?"

"I just didn't know … I didn't know it was possible, that's all."

"You should know by now that nothing is impossible for the Awakened," Aliyah said.

Sage offered Arthur a regal look before dropping to all fours. "My sister's not the only one with a few tricks up her sleeve."

"Run hard," Mr. Staples said. "Every single thing within the Quagmire will be trying to kill us. The air itself could turn poisonous if we stay in the same place too long. Try to stay away from the trees, and keep together."

Arthur scanned the Quagmire. *The whole thing is trees!*

Mr. Staples raised his sword. "For the Author and the hope of all living things!" he shouted.

The others echoed his call. "For the Author and the hope of all living things!"

Arthur embraced his Soulprint as he lurched into a run and raced into the Quagmire.

Chapter 10

THE WRONG
THING FOR THE
RIGHT REASON

Jack lay flat on a rock gazing down at his hometown. Ballylesson was nestled in a valley between two rolling hills and had once been surrounded by farms. But King Edward had been right; Jack's home had been transformed. It reminded him of the City of Shadows, except it lacked the gold and gemstones to cover the rot and decay.

Shadows slithered at the edges of his vision, and there were far more beasts and monsters walking the streets than humans. The humans who remained were filthy and looked beaten down. The low-hanging sun bathed the once sleepy town in golden light, yet there was no beauty left in Ballylesson. Anger burned in Jack as he searched the once familiar streets.

Thick webs covered every street and building. The webbing was black as pitch, and all of it could be traced back to a single pool of darkness. *That's where I stabbed the Assassin,* Jack realized. The webbing spread from the place the Assassin's blood had first spilled.

Monsters and beasts walked in and out of O'flannigans, Ballylesson's central store. Besides the shadowed webs, every building in town seemed to be crumbling even as Jack watched. Plaster walls were pockmarked with decay, and shutters had dropped from windows. A putrid smell wafted from the town.

"So, what do you think?" Honi asked. "How do you plan to retrieve Mrs. Dumphry's prize."

"I really don't see why Mrs. Dumphry wanted me to lead this mission," Jack said for the third time. "Surely it should be you!"

"You are one of the Children of Prophecy, and you are meant to lead the Awakened into the Last Battle. I will offer my counsel if I feel it will be helpful, but in the end the decision belongs to you."

"But why would the Awakened want me to lead?" Jack had been wondering about this for some time. "Doesn't the prophecy say Alexia and I will destroy the world? Doesn't that mean the Awakened will be destroyed? I've seen the way everyone looks at us. I know they're afraid."

"Yes"—Honi nodded—"but doesn't the prophecy also say that you are the only hope for the world? And doesn't it say that the two of you will defeat the Assassin forever?"

"But how can all of it be true?"

"How indeed," Honi said. "Death is not something to be feared. It is merely the beginning of a new adventure. Sometimes life can only be found on the other side of death." Honi searched the ground. "Do you see this acorn?"

Jack nodded.

"The mighty oak comes from an acorn that first died and was buried in the ground. Only when the acorn dies can new life spring from it." Honi turned his eyes to the ruined farms surrounding Ballylesson. "And what does a farmer do to his fields every few years to ensure his crops stay strong?"

"He burns them," Jack said.

"That's right. Every few years the land must be burned. The old and worn must die so it can be replaced by the new and strong. Just because the prophecy says you and Alexia will destroy us does not mean you are evil. Many do not understand these things. And people fear what they don't understand. But fear is nothing more than an empty suit of armor."

Honi tossed the acorn aside, then clapped his hands together. "Now, what is your plan, young Master Staples? How do we fetch Mrs. Dumphry's prize and get safely away?"

"I was thinking we should just walk in and take it," Jack said. He'd thought long and hard, and it was the only thing that made sense. "I think we wear the black cloaks we brought and walk down the main street and into the schoolhouse. We haven't seen anyone come or go from there since we arrived, so there's a good chance it's empty." Jack was breathless by the end. He wondered if Honi might burst out laughing at the stupidity of the plan.

Honi scrunched his brow in thought before finally letting out a long breath. "Remarkable!" He clapped his hands together. "It is obvious Mrs. Dumphry was right to place you in charge of this mission. It is a brilliant plan."

Jack felt his cheeks grow warm. He pulled the black-and-silver cloak from his bag and climbed into it, then crawled down from the edge of the rise and stood fully upright. "Should we go now?" he asked.

"I don't know. What do you think?"

"Yes …" Jack felt his cheeks growing warm again. "Yes, I think that might be best."

"Brilliant," Honi muttered. "Absolutely brilliant."

Alexia turned a corner, then skidded to a stop, barely suppressing a scream. A Shadule was slithering up the stairwell toward them. The creature was so close, she'd nearly stepped on it. The Shadule hissed as it rose.

"Your Highness,"—the creature bowed its head—"I did not expect to find you here. Are you not meant to be with the Shadow Lord in the arena?" A look of shock passed over the creature's face, and it bonelessly darted forward and wrapped its hands around Parker's neck. "My lady!" the Shadule rasped. "This boy is a Light Eyes! I must kill him now!"

Alexia paused. *It thinks I'm me from the past!*

Parker gasped for breath as he stared wide-eyed at the Shadule. Alexia made her voice hard. "Who are you to question the High Princess of Thaltorose? I command you to let him go!"

The Shadule still hovered over Parker, but it loosened its grip as it eyed Alexia warily.

"I was watching the games, and I grew bored." She stepped forward. "But I do not answer to you, worm. Or do you want me to tell Belial of your insubordination?"

The Shadule let go of Parker so it could kneel before her. "No, Highness," it whimpered. "Please. There is no need to tell the master. I was merely concerned for your well-being. This boy is a Light Eyes, and he is dangerous."

Parker probed at the fresh bruises on his neck.

"We shall see," Alexia said. "I may allow you to make it up to me, worm. There is something I would have you do."

"Anything, Mistress, anything you ask," the creature sniveled.

"When I was last down here, I saw a door covered in chains held by a thick lock. On the door was a carving of a bird surrounded by notes of music. Do you know of such a door?"

The Shadule glanced at her cautiously. "Yes, High Princess, I know of the door."

"Tell me, is it what I think it is? Are there Myzerahls in there?"

"Yes. It is a nest. But the birds are dangerous. It really would be best to stay away from."

"I need the key to the lock," Alexia said.

The Shadule looked longingly up the stairwell. A beastly roar sounded from above. *No,* Alexia thought. *They're waking up! We're running out of time.* "Find me the key, now."

The Shadule fished a key from somewhere beneath its second skin, then offered it to Alexia. "Please, High Princess, I beg your forgiveness. I will serve you in all things!"

Alexia remembered her first days in the city. Her uncle had told her that every dark servant would live or die at her command. His exact words were, *"Tell any citizen of Thaltorose or any member of the Shadow Army to stop breathing—and they will."*

"You must know that forgiveness cannot exist in the Shadow Army." Alexia felt a chill run down her spine. "You have failed Belial, and you have failed me. I command you to stop breathing."

The Shadule's pale eyes opened wide. It backed away fearfully. "No!" it shrieked. "Have mercy. I beg you!"

"You will do as I command, or Belial will deal with you. And you can be sure that death at his hands will be far worse than death at mine."

The Shadule groaned, then melted to the ground. It didn't take long for it to begin to asphyxiate, and Alexia felt sick to her stomach. The Shadule began to thrash in front of her, suffocating at her command. When Parker placed a hand on her shoulder, she saw a mixture of fear and shock on his face.

"Do you think I'm wrong?" Alexia couldn't keep the tears from her eyes as she stared at the dying Shadule.

"I know they hurt you," Parker said, "but, yes, I think this is wrong. I don't know what the difference is between killing it in battle and killing it this way, but it doesn't feel right."

"And do you think this creature would care about what's right if it were in our position? Do you think the Assassin will make it a fair fight?"

"No." Parker's eyes never left the thrashing Shadule. "But we're meant to be better than them."

Alexia watched another few seconds, then nodded sharply. "Breathe," she commanded.

The creature gasped as it inhaled. "Thank you, Princess. I will not fail you again, I swear it."

"I want you to find the darkest prison cell and lock yourself in it," Alexia said. "No matter what you see or hear, you will not come out of the prison until I command you to do so. Do you understand?"

"Yes, High Princess," the Shadule hissed. "Thank you." It slithered down the stairs and disappeared.

Alexia watched it leave. "We could have ended it," she said, "but now it will live to fight us another day."

"True," Parker said. "But we didn't sink to its level. Father always said there is no difference between someone who does the wrong thing for the wrong reasons and someone who does the wrong thing for the right reasons. There's no such thing as the lesser of two evils."

Alexia nodded. She hated the idea of leaving the Shadule alive, but the cold feeling that had been forming in her stomach was gone. *I don't want to be like them.* "Making the right choice should feel easier, shouldn't it?" she said.

"Maybe. But if it was, wouldn't everyone do it?"

"I suppose that makes sense."

"What did you want with the key? And what is a Myzerahl?" Parker asked.

"It's a bird. We were attacked by one of them in the woods just outside London. When it sings, your greatest fears come to life. And though I have no idea if it will work, I want to use the Myzerahls to help free the prisoners. But we have to capture some of them first."

Arthur could barely breathe. Every step in the Quagmire was exhausting. Sage galloped alongside him on all fours; she moved like a tiger. Her eyes had turned yellow, and a long tail flowed behind her. Aliyah flittered just above them.

King Edward followed close behind, and Mr. Staples led the way. They'd never have made it this far without Mr. Staples. The man was unbelievable with the sword, but it was his Soulprints that kept them alive. Each time they became bogged down, Mr. Staples would spin and send out into the Quagmire a vortex of … something. Like silver bullets. And where the bolts hit, the Quagmire retreated. When evil struck, Mr. Staples became transparent for just a moment so the attackers flowed right through him.

Each step brought a deadly attack, and Arthur was quickly discovering new ways to use his Soulprint. Vines wrapped around his ankles and body, but he sliced through them. When a tree attacked, Arthur forged the light into a battering ram and slammed it into the tree, sending it staggering back. In newly formed quicksand, he molded his light into a platform that lifted him upward and flowed beneath the feet of his four friends. An earthquake struck and a crevasse opened beneath them, but Arthur's platform kept them from being swallowed.

Arthur dove away from a large boulder that tumbled out of nowhere. It crashed past as he rolled to his feet. More boulders came, but King Edward took care of most. He jumped about like a madman, punching through the rocks as if they were as light as air.

Still, with each passing second, the Awakened were losing momentum. It wasn't just nature that was trying to stop them; it was the swarms of bugs, the animals, and the air itself.

More than once Aliyah saved Arthur from a winged beast he hadn't seen coming. She flittered about, sending arrow after arrow into the enemy. Her razored wings also acted as a weapon; anything that touched them was sliced to ribbons.

Arthur used his Soulprint to help Mr. Staples clear a path. He cut and battered and slammed the enemy with his light, but the world was against them. Each time he helped Mr. Staples, he was vulnerable to an attack from behind.

Sage snarled and leaped on a lion-like beast. In one smooth motion, she sunk newly formed claws into its back, then rolled over and hurled it away without slowing. Arthur couldn't dance as he ran, but when he saw a tree blocking the way, he managed to spin and send a horizontal wall of sharp light shooting just over Mr. Staples's head.

Lava shot from the ground on either side, burning holes through Arthur's platform. He quickly filled in the holes and molded a thick umbrella of light to keep the lava from hitting them on the way down. Behind him, King Edward slammed his fist into a tree that had come too close. The tree shattered, though not before another tree had wrapped the king in thick roots. Arthur cut the roots with his light, then staggered to a stop.

"We're here," Mr. Staples called. "Watch my back as I dig."

Aliyah landed on the rock just above Mr. Staples. "We'll hold them off," she said, "but hurry."

Arthur turned. The path they had cleared was gone. Swarms of insects, winged creatures, beasts, and trees opposed them. Arthur strengthened the platform and clenched his fists. And then the air thinned.

Chapter 11

I AM SPECIAL

Night had fallen by the time Jack and Honi entered Ballylesson. They walked down the main street in the dim light of a full moon. He and Honi had rubbed ashes on their clothes and faces so they could blend in.

"It might be best if we slouch a little as well," Honi whispered.

Jack nodded. He couldn't stop himself from glancing at the men and women around him. He hadn't recognized anyone, but he was curious as to who might still be there. His breath caught when he saw a man stumbling toward him. *Doctor Falvey?* Jack could barely believe it. The doctor had always been kind. *Surely only evil men would serve the Assassin!* The doctor's eyes were dull and listless.

Jack slowed his walk. Everyone had the same lifeless step. It was as if they were only walking because it was what one did, not because they were going somewhere. He glanced inside O'flannigans as he plodded past. A Shadule stood in the center of the store with wings outstretched. Monsters cowered as it hissed orders.

Though Jack tried not to step on the shadowed webs crisscrossing the street, there were places the webbing was so thick, he had no choice—and every time, something changed. He never stayed still long enough to figure out what, but he could feel it.

"Get out of my way!" someone shouted.

Jack turned to see Doctor Falvey yelling at another man. *It's Farmer McNally!* Both men stood in thick patches of shadowed webbing. The doctor grabbed a knife from inside his cloak and stabbed the old farmer in the shoulder. McNally gasped, and when his blood dripped to the ground, it hissed and popped like oil in a frying pan.

"I warn you," the doctor shouted. "Get in my way again, and it'll be the last thing you do!"

Farmer McNally whimpered as he stumbled away holding his bloody shoulder.

"It is far worse than I'd imagined," Honi whispered. "Did you see the farmer's blood when it hit the ground?"

"Yes," Jack said. "What does it mean?"

"As I was telling you before, blood has power." Honi's eyes stayed glued to the spot where the blood had landed. The farmer's blood was mingling with the shadowed darkness as the webbing thickened. "Those who choose to serve the Assassin will eventually be transformed into his image," Honi said. "I fear that those who follow him are changing. Their flesh is being corrupted as they take on his image."

Jack was horrified as he stared at the webbing covering the town. "Is all of it blood?"

"Yes"—Honi nodded—"though I'm sure most of it is the Assassin's. Unless we can find a way to stop it, the blood will continue to spread until it covers the world."

The two made their way toward the schoolhouse. "Is it possible for the Assassin to kill the Author?" Jack whispered.

"I don't know," Honi said, "but it may be possible to destroy the Author's greatest work. If the Assassin can convince humankind to follow him, he will have won the war. And if he can transform humans into his image, he will have broken the Author's heart. We humans are unlike anything in the entire universe. We have the blood of the Author in our veins. And that is why the Assassin hates us. He won't stop until every last one of us has become like the poor souls who walk these streets."

When he saw the schoolhouse, Jack wanted to scream. The shadowed blood covered the school completely. He felt cold.

"I thought this might be the case," Honi said. "Mrs. Dumphry's school would have been of great importance to the Assassin. He would do all in his power to destroy something she loved."

"I think it might be best if only one of us enters," Jack said. "Mrs. Dumphry wanted me to lead, so I should go. You keep watch."

"I think that is a wise plan. But be careful in there."

"I'm sorry. I didn't mean to tell you what to do." Jack suddenly felt foolish. "You can do as you like—"

"A leader does not apologize for giving instruction," Honi said. "And only a fool spurns wisdom. I am old, Jack Staples. I rarely act the fool. As I said, it is a good plan."

In many ways the old man reminded Jack of Mrs. Dumphry. He gazed into the schoolhouse. Thick webs covered everything, floor to ceiling. He took a deep breath, then stepped inside. As he entered, shadowed tendrils detached from the floorboards and slithered up his leg.

Click. The key turned in the enormous lock as chains dropped to the floor. Parker shoved them aside, then grabbed a torch from the wall.

"Remember," Alexia said again, "whatever you see is not real. Mrs. Dumphry said the only way to defeat a Myzerahl is to face your fears. But if we give in, even for a second, we'll die." Alexia placed her hands on the door. "She also told us not to look back. She said no matter what you hear, don't look back. I don't know why, but I think it's important."

"And you're sure we need these birds?" Parker asked.

"Without the Myzerahls, we have no chance of saving anyone."

"All right, then. I'm ready if you are."

The battle in the streets above echoed through the corridors. Alexia wanted to run up and help fight the Assassin, but she knew there was nothing she could do. The Awakened would be defeated in a few hours.

She shoved open the door, and they stepped inside, then pushed the door closed. Parker held the torch high in the darkness. Thick branches and twigs covered the floor and walls, with bits of leaves and dirt stuffed between. They began to walk deeper into the branches.

"It's like—" Parker brought the torch low.

"Like we're in a nest," Alexia said.

Parker held the torch high. "What do you think those are for?"

Alexia had just noticed the thick steel crates stacked back near the door. "I don't know," she said. "Maybe that's how we get them out of here."

A small bird fluttered past Alexia's face, then disappeared into the darkness. Then many more birds rocketed out of the darkness, slamming their bodies into Parker and Alexia. The children ducked and screamed. Again and again the small birds pummeled them with their bodies. The only sound was the beating of their wings and the screams of the two children.

Alexia stumbled into the darkness. Once she escaped the pool of light, the birds left her alone, even as they redoubled their attacks on Parker.

"It's the torch!" she yelled. "They don't like the torch! Drop it and follow the sound of my voice!" Thousands of birds fluttered in and out of the light, clobbering Parker.

Parker dropped the torch and stumbled toward her, but he disappeared in the darkness.

"Parker!" Alexia cried. "Are you there?" The only sound was Alexia's terrified breathing. "Parker, I'm here!"

Nothing. Terror formed in the pit of her belly as thousands of birds began to sing. The song that filled the darkness was slow and steady, but it was growing louder by the second. The birds began to harmonize.

Alexia ran, then stumbled. *Alone!* As had happened so often in her life, everyone had either abandoned her or been taken from her. The darkness was never ending. She lurched forward again, tripped again. The Myzerahls' song vibrated in her chest.

She began to weep as she beat at the ground with her fists. "What's wrong with me?" she screamed. "Why do I always end up alone? Why does everyone I love have to die?"

"Because you are cursed."

Alexia gasped. She stood slowly, afraid of what she would see when she turned around. Was it a Shadule, like the last time she was caught in the Myzerahls' song? Was it her father or mother screaming at her? Alexia turned to see a man bathed in eerie light. He was sitting on a plush chair with one leg hanging lazily over the side.

Alexia brushed at her tears. The Myzerahls still sang, though she barely noticed. "Who are you? What do you want with me? What do you mean I'm cursed?"

"Don't you recognize me?" The man smiled wickedly.

Alexia blinked. He wore strange clothes and a colorful patchwork cloak. She'd seen him before, but where? "You're the poet!" According to the Awakened, the poet was the Author made flesh. He was the creator of all things, and he was sitting in front of her.

"I knew it would come to you eventually." The poet leaned forward. "You asked what was wrong with you, why everyone you love has been taken away. And this is the answer: you are cursed. Your birth ruined everything. The world needed Jack. He is the one who will destroy the Assassin, not you." The poet shook his head. "To put it simply, you were a mistake. You are not needed. You never have been." The poet stood, then stepped forward. Alexia wanted to run, but fear rooted her to the ground. "When you die, the curse will die with you."

Alexia shook her head. Each word he spoke was like a whip to her back. "No!" Her knees weakened, but she made herself stand. The song of the Myzerahls rose toward its disastrous crescendo.

"Didn't Jack have someone to watch over him?" the poet said. "Didn't he have someone protecting him every day of his life? Where were your protectors? Why didn't they find you when your parents died? Why weren't they searching for you when you joined the circus? If you are truly special, someone would have found you. But you are not. You are a curse. And I have come to fix this ... mistake!" The poet's lip curled as he drew a gleaming sword.

The Myzerahls' song was dizzying. Ten thousand songbirds flitted around her, and Alexia could feel herself fading. The poet raised his sword.

"No. You are not the poet," she said. "And I won't listen to you!"

The poet hesitated.

"I've been afraid of being alone for as long as I can remember, and I blamed myself for my parents' death, but I was just a child!"

The poet stepped back; Alexia stepped forward.

"I am special, and I am one of the Children of Prophecy. I am no mistake!" She was shaking angrily. "And though you look like him, you are not the poet. You are nothing more than the fears of a little girl." Alexia could feel her fear leaking to the floor.

The poet screamed as light burst from his eyes and mouth. And when it faded, he was gone, and only a small, warbling bird remained.

Parker stood a short distance away with the flaming torch in his hands. He was shaking. "She didn't want me," he said. "Mother didn't even want to know me. She tried to kill me."

"It wasn't real."

"That doesn't mean it didn't hurt."

She nodded. Though she was exhausted, there was something else. She'd found strength she hadn't known was there. "Come on," she said. "We need to capture as many of these birds as we possibly can. Let's go find those crates."

Chapter 12

WHO LOVES YOU, JACK?

Exhausted was far too feeble a word to explain how Arthur felt. He'd passed the point of exhaustion almost an hour ago. He danced at the base of the mountain with watery muscles. He'd sent a thousand bolts of lightning to strike tree, ground, beast, and mountain. He'd formed a platform for the Awakened to stand on, but the earth rolled so violently, it was still impossible to stand upright.

King Edward didn't stand on the platform; he leaped about like a madman, smashing fists and feet into every tree, boulder, or beast that came too close. The king seemed to have endless strength and energy.

Sage and Aliyah fought together. Aliyah flew between the trees, sending streams of arrows into anything that attacked from above. Sage ran below, leaping onto large creatures and hurling them away.

Mr. Staples was digging for the coffer and fighting against whatever evil managed to sneak past the others. The mountain trembled and shook, sending boulders crashing down. Arthur's shield of liquid light stopped most of them, but—

"I have it!" Mr. Staples yelled.

Arthur watched Jack's father tuck the coffer inside his cloak. *It's too late,* he thought. It had been more than two hours since they'd entered the Quagmire. They'd fought boldly, but getting out was going to prove impossible.

Jack shivered as he entered the schoolhouse. It was cold inside, and it took a moment for his eyes to adjust to the darkness. He felt something slithering up his legs, but when he looked, he couldn't see anything.

He glanced back to see Honi standing in the doorway and was immediately irritated. *Why does the old man have to look so smug?* he thought. *And why am I doing all the hard work while he just stands there?*

Jack knelt behind the desk as the slithering darkness swirled around him. "What are you doing just standing there?" he called to Honi. "Why don't you come help me?"

Honi leaned in but didn't enter. "Are you sure that's wise?" he asked. "Mightn't it be better if we stick to the plan?"

Jack stood. "You told me I was in charge," he shouted. "Now do as I command!"

Honi stiffened but didn't enter. "Are you feeling all right?"

"What are you good for, old man? What are you even doing here if you can't listen to a single order?" Jack placed a hand on Ashandar's hilt. "I don't need your help."

Honi raised his hands. "Jack, listen to me. I'm not sure what's happening, but this isn't you talking."

Jack drew his sword. He couldn't remember the last time he'd been this angry. "What kind of stupid name is 'Honi' anyway?" He moved toward the door and raised Ashandar.

When he stepped into the moonlight, Honi gasped. "Look, Jack! The Assassin's corruption has attached itself to you! This isn't you talking; you need to fight it!"

Jack glanced down. The old man was right. Thin, shadowed tendrils slithered all over his body. They were wriggling beneath his clothes and sinking into his skin. Part of him was horrified, but mostly he was just angry. *How dare the old man speak to me like this!* Jack swung Ashandar wildly.

Honi stepped aside, then punched Jack hard in the nose. The next thing Jack knew, he was being dragged away from the schoolhouse by his feet.

"Lemme go!" he screamed. "I'm going to make you pay, do you hear me?"

Honi didn't stop until he was safely in the schoolyard. Jack thrashed and kicked on the ground, consumed by rage. All he wanted was to hurt Honi, who knelt beside him, tearing the tendrils from his body.

Jack slowly regained control of himself. His rage subsided, and in its place was shock. "What just happened?" He rubbed his temples as he sat upright.

Honi let out a shuddering breath. "No wonder everyone we walked past was so angry," he said. "As I was telling you before, the Assassin's blood is corrupt. The rage you felt came from him." Honi turned his eyes toward the schoolhouse. "I'm afraid it will be far harder to fetch Mrs. Dumphry's prize than we imagined."

Jack shuddered. The rage had been real. It hadn't made sense to be so angry, but he hadn't cared.

Alexia didn't make a sound as the Shadule threw her Gang of Rogues into the prison cell. All looked weary beyond words and carried multiple wounds. She stayed safely hidden in the darkened corner of the cell, barely able to contain her excitement.

"The master will come for you soon," the Shadule rasped. "You will beg for death by the time he is done."

None of her gang protested as the Shadule closed the prison door. Juno dropped to the cold, wet floor and cradled Adeline's head in her lap. Adeline was bleeding from a wound in her shoulder. Josiah stared blankly at the closed door as Summer and Benaiah sat beside him. All five were filthy and streaked in blood. Some of the blood was theirs; much of it was not.

Alexia waited until she was sure the Shadule was gone, then stepped out from the darkness. "I know you are weary," she said boldly, "but if you are willing to help me, I can get you out of here. And with your help, we can free every last prisoner and animal."

None of the children so much as moved.

"I don't …" Josiah stopped. "We saw you fly away."

"I did," Alexia said with a grin, "but that was weeks ago. I've come from the past to rescue you." Alexia motioned to Parker, who stepped out of the shadows to stand beside her. "This is Parker Staples. He'll help us. But before we free the prisoners, I'm going to need your help with something else." Alexia was giddy with excitement. "We're going to free my mother."

All five children sat watching silently. Finally Juno laid Adeline's head carefully on the stone and stood. Without warning she balled her fist and slugged Alexia.

"Today was the second time you left us," Juno said. "You fled the city with your friends and left us here to rot."

Alexia flinched at her words. They hurt far more than any punch. She'd hoped her friends would be excited to see her, not angry.

"And now you dare ask for our help?" Juno was a head shorter than Alexia, but fierce.

"You're right about the first part," Alexia said carefully. "I will do everything in my power to earn back your trust. But I can't change the past. And I didn't abandon you a few hours ago. I was rescued and you weren't. I had no choice in that. But I'm here now. I've come back for you. I do need your help—not just to save my mother. I have a plan to rescue every prisoner and Clear Eyes in this city."

Juno's eyes narrowed as she studied Alexia.

"She's right." Josiah palmed bleary eyes. "It wasn't her fault that she escaped and we didn't. That anyone got away is a miracle. And she came back. That's what matters."

Alexia remembered what she'd been feeling that day. *It was today, not weeks ago. They are hungry and heartbroken and exhausted,* she reminded herself.

"Parker and I brought some food, and we'll find bandages for your wounds. For now, get something to eat and try to sleep. We'll talk when you wake."

Juno took the bag from Parker and dug inside. She handed a loaf of crusty bread to Addy, then handed out more to the others. A few minutes later, all five members of Alexia's Gang of Rogues were asleep on the dungeon floor.

"No matter what you're feeling, you must fight it," Honi repeated.

Jack nodded. "But it feels so real. When I was in there, all I wanted to do was hurt you. And it felt right."

"I'm sure it did." Honi smiled. "I had a very bad temper as a young man, and I always felt justified. Then one day I met Mrs. Dumphry. She taught me that anger is almost always unwarranted. All of our interactions, all of our decisions must come from a place of love. Love conquers anger every time."

Jack liked Honi. Though he was thousands of years younger than Mrs. Dumphry, he was still far wiser than Jack. "All right," Jack said, "I think I'm ready."

Jack closed his eyes and listened. He was beginning to understand that his sound was always there; he just needed to train his ears to hear it. He slowed his breathing. *There!* He smiled as his note rose around him. He flew backward, landing on his knees beside Mrs. Dumphry's desk. Though it had saved him only a few steps, every second mattered.

The floor was so layered in webbing, he had to puncture through the shadows to touch the floor. Even as his fingers slid along the floorboards, his anger grew. *Come on!* It was a frantic thought. *Why couldn't Mrs. Dumphry have told me which corner of the desk she hid it under?*

When he couldn't find a loose board, he crawled to the opposite side of the desk. *Stupid old hag! It's like she didn't want me to find it!* Even as the thoughts formed, he knew they were wrong, but his blood still boiled.

"There," he mumbled as the tips of his fingers found an edge. He picked at the floorboard with his fingernails, prying upward. It began to rise, then dropped again as his fingers slipped. "No!" he screamed. "Stupid board!" He slammed his fist into the desk and was immediately enraged at the pain in his hand.

"Jack! You must fight it! This is an attack as sure as any blade."

Jack had forgotten all about Honi. "Who do you think you are?" he snarled. "You are useless, old man. You are—"

"Who loves you, Jack?"

The question took him by surprise. "What are you talking about?" he growled.

"Tell me about the people who love you most. Tell me about the things you are most grateful for."

A picture of Arthur Greaves formed in his mind as Jack reached for Ashandar. Arthur was the most loyal friend anyone could have.

"Tell me, what are you thinking?" Honi said urgently.

"Arthur Greaves," Jack said through gritted teeth. "He is my friend." Jack felt something detach from his neck and drop to the floor.

"And who else? Who else are you thankful for? Who loves you?"

Jack turned back to the desk. "Alexia," he said. "Even though she was upset with me the last time I saw her, I know she loves me. She's my sister." He began prying at the floorboards again. Rage stirred inside him, but he kept talking.

"My father," he grunted. "He loves me, as does Parker. And my mother loved me enough to die for me." Jack removed the board, then stuck his entire arm into the slithering hole. The more he spoke, the more shadows slipped from his body. *There!* His hand closed around a small tin. He grabbed it and stood, looking for Honi, but the old man was no longer watching from the doorway.

Jack quickly walked toward the exit. He knew it would be safer to time travel, but the more he spoke, the more something changed inside him. It wasn't just the shadows that withered and dropped from his body; it was more. Not all of his anger came from the Assassin's blood. Somewhere deep inside, Jack had been angry for a long time. As he spoke words of gratefulness and love, much of his anger melted away.

"And I'm grateful for you, Honi," he said. "Thank you for being willing to follow me and help me." Where Jack walked, the shadows fled. He stopped, shocked. Honi lay on the ground with three older boys standing over him. Jack couldn't tell if he was still breathing.

"Well looky, looky." Jonty Dobson cracked his knuckles and stepped over Honi's body. "It's Jack Staples. And where is the other one? Where is that fat little boy who's always by your side? Where is little piggy?"

Even as Jack raised Ashandar, he couldn't imagine using it against Jonty or the others. No matter how wicked they might be, they were only boys.

"Hello, Jonty." Jack tried to sound both confident and dangerous. "Why am I not surprised to find you here?"

"The entire Shadow Army is looking for you," Jonty said, "and you come here with nothing but an old man? You are either incredibly stupid, or you're looking for something important. Which is it? What were you doing in the schoolhouse?"

Jack resisted the urge to reach for the tin he'd tucked safely inside his coat pocket. He ignored Jonty's question and stepped forward. His hands warmed around Ashandar, and he assumed a very dangerous stance. The blade called to him, willing him to move. But Jack didn't listen. He would not hurt another human, not if he could help it. "You may find I'm not as easy a target as I once was," he replied levelly. "I will give you one chance to run. Leave now and take your friends with you."

All of the boys snickered, and the largest hefted a thick spear. Jonty stepped back and glanced at his friends. "Put your weapons down," he said. "He's not going to fight us."

"You aren't in charge here," an older boy said. "Why shouldn't we fight him?"

Jonty bent low and placed his knife against Honi's throat.

"No. Jonty, please!" Ashandar vibrated in Jack's hands.

"The Awakened care about their own," Jonty said. "It's their most glaring weakness." He met Jack's eyes as he pressed the blade deeper into Honi's skin. "Drop your sword now."

Jack hesitated only a moment before dropping Ashandar.

"That's better." Jonty's eyes flicked to his friends. "See, I told you we wouldn't need to fight him. Search his pockets and tie him up."

The two boys lowered their weapons and stepped forward. The moment their backs were to Jonty, he leaped at them and kicked, punched, and bludgeoned both boys until they lay unconscious at his feet. Jack watched in confused horror as Jonty rose and stepped close. He had a mad look in his eyes, and spittle dripping from his chin.

"I didn't kill them!" he said. "I promised I wouldn't hurt anyone. But I had to stop them, or they would have taken you. You have to tell them I kept my promise!"

"What are you talking about? Who do I have to tell?"

Jonty wiped his chin with the back of his hand and dropped the knife. He placed Honi on his shoulder like a sack of grain. "We need to go before anyone sees."

Jonty scurried to the edge of the woods, then turned and made a tsking sound. He nodded in the direction of the woods before disappearing into the darkness.

Jack followed. He didn't have a choice. Jonty had taken Honi. When he caught up, Jonty began to whine. "They have to help me now. You all do. I saved you! They would have killed you for sure. So now you have to take me with you, right?"

"What's going on?" Jack demanded.

Jonty squealed and dropped to the ground as a hulking figure stepped out from behind a tree a few paces in front of him. "Please don't hurt me. Please! I saved them! You'll see!"

Jack unsheathed Ashandar and raised the blade warily.

"That's no way to greet a friend!"

Jack spun excitedly. He knew that voice. "Wild!"

His friend stood with an arrow half nocked. "Hello, Jack!"

"It be good to be seeing you again!" Andreal rumbled from behind him.

"Andreal! I can't believe you're both here!" Jack grinned. "How on earth are the two of you in Ballylesson?"

"Please don't hurt me!" Jonty lay prostrate at their feet. "I didn't want them to hurt the old man. They were going to kill him, but I told them to knock him unconscious. I saved his life! I haven't failed you. You must see it!" Jonty began to sob.

"Quit yer snivelin." Andreal let out a loud harrumph. "I do no like this boy." He shook his head. "But Wild would no let me be knocking him out, no matter how nicely I be asking!"

Jonty whimpered as Wild chuckled.

Chapter 13

WHERE SHADOWS LIVE

The small band of Awakened stumbled away from the base of the mountain. Arthur was so weary, he could barely think. Attacks came from every direction. Thousands of bugs swarmed and bit as the earth rolled, trees swiped, and miniature tornadoes spun wildly past. Boulders crashed even as fearsome creatures attacked with razor claws, teeth, and beaks.

Arthur could no longer maintain the platform of light that flowed beneath them. It kept dissipating as they staggered over the slithering ground. All the Awakened were wounded and covered in stings and bites. Sage leaped about, swiping her claws, as Aliyah fluttered just above, sending arrows into the enemy. Arthur's lungs burned as the air thinned even more.

King Edward led the charge. Every few seconds Arthur could see the king leap high from somewhere and smash some enemy aside. Arthur couldn't look back to see if Mr. Staples was still with them. All his attention was given to moving forward.

Sage screamed, cut down by a monstrous cat, and when Arthur hurled a lightning bolt, it missed—he was far too exhausted to aim. With his attention on Sage, he didn't see the vines until they'd wrapped around his waist.

"Help!" Within seconds the vines were so tight, he couldn't breathe. Sage was pinned beneath the catlike creature and screamed again. Aliyah swept down and ripped the creature away, but then a tree branch swatted her aside.

Arthur's breathing came in gasps. He tried to cut the vines away with a razor of light but couldn't maintain his Soulprint. Every time he tried to hone the light into a sharp edge, it dulled and slipped away. *This is it*, he thought. *We failed, and now we're all going to die.* The vines tensed and fell away without warning, sending Arthur tumbling to the ground. Mr. Staples stood above him with a sword in one hand and Sage thrown over his shoulder.

King Edward was also there with a gasping Aliyah on her knees beside him. The king was badly wounded, and the left side of his body had been burned, but he had a fierce look in his eyes. Mr. Staples knelt over Sage and poured a dark liquid over the wound in her shoulder. She gasped and promptly fainted.

"It has been an honor to fight by your side, Lightning Dancer," King Edward said as he pulled Arthur to his feet. Arthur wanted to collapse again.

Mr. Staples retrieved the Poet's Coffer from his cloak and quickly placed it inside Arthur's coat pocket. "Tell Jack and Parker I love them," he said. "Tell them not to mourn me, that we will see each other again on the other side of this life. Once you're out of the Quagmire, go south. It should take you four days to reach the Valley of Elah. That's where Jack and Alexia will be headed if they aren't there already."

Arthur didn't understand what was happening. He was far too tired to find a coherent thought.

"We're close to the border," Mr. Staples said. "You are strong, Arthur. Stronger than I ever thought possible. Don't give up," he said as he cut down a charging, rhino-like beast. "Now"—he shared a look with King Edward—"let us run together one last time!"

The world trembled as the king and Mr. Staples leaped forward. Aliyah rose to her feet, lurching after them. James Staples still carried Sage over his shoulder as he fought one-handed. Strange silver slivers exploded from him in an otherworldly maelstrom.

The ground softened as Arthur stumbled after them. All of his attention was given to staying on his feet and following the two men. Trees moved to cut him off, but King Edward bounded into them, swinging his fists in a fury and pressing them back. Arthur managed to mold a clumsy shield of light around himself.

The king and Mr. Staples were no longer wasting any energy protecting themselves. They were human battering rams, and their only mission was to save Arthur, Sage, and Aliyah. But there were far too many monsters. Arthur ran past as evil creatures swarmed over Jack's father. Trees overtook King Edward, who screamed as a branch wrapped around his shoulder and another snarled his leg. Arthur wept as he stumbled past—all of his energy was spent on maintaining his shield of light and putting one foot in front of the other. Between one step and the next, he shoved through a wall of slithering vines, broke free of the Quagmire, and collapsed onto the hard-packed dirt.

He turned to see the border of the Quagmire. It cut through the earth like a razor, and even as he watched, it moved steadily outward. Arthur scrambled back. "Come on!" he screamed. "You're almost there!"

Aliyah burst through. The moment she crossed the border, she crashed to the ground, rolling onto her back. She was covered in cuts and bruises but was still alive.

"Is Sage here? Did she get out?"

"Not yet," Arthur said. "It's only the two of us so far." His eyes scanned the border as Aliyah sat up beside him. "Please," he whispered. "Please!"

Aliyah's wings folded into her back as she stood beside him with fists clenched. Mr. Staples appeared. He was bloodied and burned but still carried an unconscious Sage over his shoulder. He thrust her out, then fought to break through the tangle of slithering vines. Aliyah pulled her sister to safety, and Arthur reached for Mr. Staples's hands, but before he could get a firm grasp, James Staples was yanked back in.

Arthur screamed and scrambled back from the expanding corruption. For a long moment, he stood at the edge, trembling. Turning his back on the Quagmire was the hardest thing he'd ever done, but he knew he was finished. He didn't have the strength to go back in. He walked back to Sage and Aliyah and began to weep. James Staples and King Edward had given their lives to save them.

"We can't stay here," he said. "This whole valley will be part of the Quagmire soon."

Aliyah nodded.

"I'll carry your sister," Arthur said. "But we need to get some-where safe as soon as possible. Every dark servant within one hundred leagues will be coming for us. They can feel the coffer." He knelt and lifted Sage. He was sure he couldn't walk more than a few minutes, but it would have to do. Aliyah stood by his side, and together the two children staggered up the steep canyon.

Jack glanced at Jonty Dobson as they stalked through the forest. The boy seemed frightened of his own shadow. *Why?* Jack wondered.

Andreal led the way, cradling a still unconscious Honi.

"That's all her letter said?" Wild asked. "That she wanted you to retrieve the tin?"

"Yes," Jack said. "I don't know what's in it or why she needs it. But we were to get the tin and meet her in the Valley of Elah, wherever that is."

"And you're sure Alexia's okay?" Wild asked.

"That's what my father said. I don't know any more than I've already told you. She spent some time with my father and brother, and then she and Parker ran off to rescue her mother from the City of Shadows."

"Why does she always have to be so brave?" Wild frowned. "I'm not going to be there to save her this time! Did she—" He stopped. "Did she tell your father anything about me?"

"No, I told you everything I know. And why would she …" Jack smiled. "You like her! You like Alexia!"

"No, I don't. I just … I just care about her, that's all. I mean I do like her, but not like that, or not entirely, at least. I mean—"

Jack erupted in laughter as Wild turned his attention to the surrounding woods.

"I'm not certain," Jack finally said, "but I think she might like you as well."

"Really?" Wild said.

He wore such a look of hope that Jack laughed all the harder. "The way you two are always going at each other, I thought maybe you hated her. But she treats you the same way, so maybe it is love."

"I never said love! You can't ever tell her about this, Jack!"

Jack was laughing so hard, he had to wipe away tears.

"It's really not that funny," Wild said irritably.

They walked in silence awhile before Jack changed the subject. "You still haven't told me how you and Andreal came to be here."

"We landed in a pile of hay at my uncle's barn on the outskirts of Ballylesson," Wild said. "We fell from the sky and crashed through the barn roof."

"But why did you stay? Why didn't you go to the Great Oasis, or somewhere?" Jack asked.

"Because every time we thought about leaving, it felt wrong. It's as if the Author wanted us to be here."

"I've heard Mrs. Dumphry say that kind of thing before," Jack said, "but I've never understood it. How do you know the Author wanted you to stay?"

Wild shrugged. "It's not like I hear him talking or anything; it's more like a feeling I can't shake or a voice inside my heart. Andreal felt it too. Once we even tried to leave, but after a few hours, we turned around and came back."

"How long have you been here?"

"Four months."

"But you didn't even know why you were here. You could have waited forever."

"But we didn't," Wild said. "Now that we've found you, it's obvious why we're here. Whatever happens next, you're going to need our help."

Jack shook his head; then his eyes landed on Jonty Dobson. "I still don't understand what he's doing here. Why is he helping us?"

"I found him a few nights ago," Wild said. "He was crying behind the schoolhouse. I felt bad for him, so I told him he could join the Awakened and fight with us. But he thought I was trying to trick him. I told him if he changed his mind, he could find me in the western woods. But we would only take him in if he stopped hurting people."

"Will you still let me join the Awakened?" Jonty asked. "If I hadn't knocked the old man out, they would have killed him. So I had to hurt him. You must believe me!"

"I believe you," Wild said. "And, yes, you can join us, if you wish."

"But how do I do it? Do I need to hurt someone first?"

Jack and Wild shared a horrified look. "Of course not!" Wild said.

"I don't want to hurt anybody." Jonty's voice raised an octave. "But I'll do what I must. If you want me to prove myself, I will! Just take me with you. I can't stay here any longer!"

"You don't have to do anything to join the Awakened," Jack said. "It's not like that. You just have to believe. I mean, I guess that's it."

Wild nodded. Jonty's eyes narrowed as he stepped back and ran into Andreal.

"Watch where yer going!" the giant boomed.

Jonty cowered. "I'm sorry, master. I didn't mean to fail you. Do you wish to punish me?"

"This boy be making me sick to me stomach!" Andreal said.

"Stand up!" Jack felt sick too. *Is this what it means to be a follower of the Assassin? Why would anyone choose to stay?* "There's no bowing or scraping among the Awakened. We don't call each other master, and we definitely don't hurt people for no reason. If you want to be one of us, you're in. That's it. I'll teach you all I know of the Author as we find time, but for now I just need your help, all right?"

Jonty bowed and nodded in agreement. "As you command. What do you need me to do?"

Jack rolled his eyes. "I need to find out if Arthur Greaves's parents are still here. I promised him I would."

"Who's Arthur Greaves?" Jonty scrunched his forehead.

Jack sighed. "You know him as little piggy. I need to find out if little piggy's parents are still here."

Jonty flushed, then bowed again. "No, they left months ago when the Masters first came to town."

Jack nodded. "And what of my house? Has it also been taken over by the Shadow Souled?"

Jonty nodded. "All the houses have been taken by the Owners and Masters. The Slaves and Pawns are made to sleep in the streets or beneath the trees. We ran out of beds weeks ago, and food's been scarce for ages. Nothing seems to grow anymore, and most of the animals have become Oriax, or worse, so there's no meat to be found. I've had nothing but roots and leaves for the past week."

Jack's anger grew as he dug into his satchel to find some bread and cheese for Jonty. This was his home. Almost all of his memories came from Ballylesson. He turned to Wild and Andreal. "I'm not leaving until I've chased every dark servant out of Ballylesson. And we've got to get rid of the Assassin's blood, too." He offered both boy and giant a level look. "Will you stay and help me fight?"

Andreal let out a low whistle as Jonty began to whimper. "It's no going to be easy." The giant scratched his chin through his thick beard. "But I suppose so long as we be fighting the Shadow, it no matter where we be fighting. Aye, I will fight by yer side."

"I don't know how wise it is," Wild said, "but I'll stay. Ballylesson is my home, too."

"And so will I," Honi said. He was still cradled in Andreal's arms.

"You're awake!" Jack ran over.

"Yes, I've been awake for a few minutes now, but I was rather enjoying the ride." He winked at Andreal, who chuckled and set Honi down, propping him against a tree.

"How are you feeling?" Jack asked.

"I have been better, but I will be well soon enough." Honi rubbed his temples with the tips of his fingers. "If we are going to stay and fight this darkness, we will need an army at our backs or a brilliant plan. Which will it be?"

"I don't think we have time to raise an army," Jack said.

"Does this mean we're not leaving? You won't be taking me with you?" Jonty paled.

"Not yet." Jack placed a hand on Jonty's shoulder. "But I promise, things will be better. All we need to do is rid our home of every last bit of evil, and then we can go."

"You don't know what you're saying!" Jonty had a feverish look in his eyes. "It's not just the monsters you'll be fighting. It's the shadows. They're alive! You can't beat the Shadow Lord. Nothing can. Please, we need to leave before we're all dead, or worse!"

"This is our fight, Jonty. And now that you're one of us, his name is no longer the Shadow Lord. We call him Assassin, and we'll fight him with everything we have. This is where we'll make our stand. If we can't beat him here, we can't win anywhere."

Chapter 14

A BULLY IS A BULLY
IS A BULLY

Alexia rocked on her heels. She'd been sitting with Parker inside the cell for hours. Josiah, Juno, Summer, Benaiah, and Adeline all lay sleeping on the dungeon floor. With every passing hour, Alexia began to question her plan. How could they possibly get everyone out when Elion had been able to rescue only a handful? And what if Mrs. Dumphry was wrong? *Was* Alexia's mother here?

"I know you feel bad about leaving them behind," Parker murmured, "but you must realize there was nothing you could have done. Give them time."

"Maybe ..." Alexia shook her head. "But the Last Battle has begun. We don't have time. According to the prophecy, Jack and I are meant to destroy the world soon. And how can anyone forgive that?"

"How long have we been sleeping?" Josiah groaned as he sat up.

"Probably three or four hours now," Alexia said.

"And you've been here the whole time?"

"Most of it. We snuck out and found some more food and bandages." She stood and offered Josiah some crusty bread and mildewed cheese. "Most of the food is rotten, but this is the best of it."

Josiah grabbed it and took a bite as the rest of the Gang of Rogues began to stir. Parker offered water, bread, and cheese to each of them.

"So what's this plan you were talking about?" Josiah wiped his mouth with the back of his hand. "And what's this about your mother?"

"If she's anything like your father, we should leave her in the dungeons and be done with it," Juno said.

"Juno!" Josiah said. "I get that you're angry; we all are. But nobody deserves to be in these dungeons."

For a moment Juno met Josiah's eyes defiantly, then looked away.

"I was wrong about Korah," Alexia said. "He wasn't my father. He was my father's twin brother. And I'm not certain that my mother is here, but if she is, it was Korah who brought her. I think he captured everyone I ever cared about and threw them into these dungeons."

Juno nodded. "I'm sorry. Josiah is right. Nobody deserves to be here."

"You have every right to hate me," Alexia said. "But I hope you'll be willing to forgive what I did and let us start again. I hope—"

"You don't need to apologize again," Juno said. "We'll do whatever we can to help you save your mother and the others."

Summer, Benaiah, and Adeline all nodded.

"Thank you. Your friendship means everything to me," Alexia said. "It won't be easy, but I have a plan. How bad are your injuries? Will you be able to run when the time comes?"

"How are you feeling, Summer?" Juno asked.

"I think I'm strong enough." Summer extended her arms and turned in a slow circle. Alexia gasped as tiredness and pain drained from her body. Adeline smiled as the gash in her shoulder mended itself, and Benaiah grinned as his bruises faded.

"That was incredible!" Alexia gasped again.

"Thank you." Summer managed a tired-looking smile. She glanced at Josiah as she lay back down on the dungeon floor. "I think I need to rest awhile." Within seconds, she was asleep.

"Unfortunately, she can't heal herself," Josiah said. "And it takes a lot out of her. But, yes, it is amazing."

Alexia shared an unbelieving look with Parker. She felt as if she'd slept for days and eaten a warm meal besides. "We're going to need a lot of wax. Any idea where they store the candles?"

Benaiah nodded. "If you can get me out of here, yes."

"Good," Alexia said. "Now for the hard part. The rest of you will need to speak to the prisoners. If this plan is going to work, every one of them will need to know about it beforehand."

Josiah scratched his chin in thought. "I'd bet most of them are back in the dirt. The Shadule wanted us handy so it could question us."

Most of the prisoners weren't kept inside dungeons. They were made to crawl into small mounds dug into the dirt, which worked both as a prison and a grave. If the Awakened died while in the mounds, their bodies were sealed inside.

"Adeline, if we can get you in the middle of them, do you think you can work your trick?" Josiah asked.

"Just tell me what they need to know, and I'll do my best," Adeline said.

"What trick?" Alexia asked. But Adeline just smiled at her. "Wait, how did you just …?" Adeline hadn't said a word, yet her voice had sounded in Alexia's mind. Alexia laughed. "That will come in very handy indeed."

"Where are we?" Sage croaked. Her eyes were open.

"I don't know," Arthur whispered. He knelt beside her, gazing into a valley. "But don't talk too loud. There's some kind of army camped just below. It's too dark to see if they're Awakened or Shadow Souled." Sweat poured from Arthur, and his arms and shoulders burned like fire. Carrying Sage for so long had taken the last energy he had. Now that they'd stopped, he was certain he wouldn't be able to pick her up again.

Sage groaned. "How long have I been out?"

"We left the Quagmire two days ago," Aliyah whispered.

Arthur dropped to his back as the world seemed to spin.

Sage sat up with a look of surprise. "And he's been carrying me?"

Aliyah nodded as she offered her sister a skin of water. "I've never seen anything like it. I'm so tired I can hardly stand, but Arthur carried you every step of the way. And we've barely stopped since leaving the Quagmire."

Arthur was far too tired to be embarrassed. In truth, he was also surprised they'd made it so far. He suspected his endurance might have had something to do with the Poet's Coffer. The box was warm against his chest and seemed to radiate energy.

"And what of King Edward and Mr. Staples?" Sage searched the surrounding darkness.

"You don't remember?" Aliyah asked.

Sage rubbed her eyes. "I don't remember much."

"They gave their lives to get us out," Aliyah said. "We've been running ever since."

Sage exhaled a long breath. "I can't believe it," she whispered. She struggled to her feet and gazed into the valley below. "And the coffer?"

"Arthur has it. Mr. Staples gave it to him just before he died."

"You both stay here," Sage said. "You've already done the impossible. I'm going to find out who's camped below."

It took Arthur a moment to understand her words, and by the time he did, she was already gone. *No, it's not safe!* The thought formed slowly. *It must be the Assassin's army. Why would the Awakened be gathering in the middle of nowhere?* Yet he was far too exhausted to move. He closed his eyes and fell into a deep sleep.

When Arthur opened his eyes, he saw a man kneeling over him with a torch in his hand. Sage stood beside him. Arthur tried to speak, but nothing came. He was dimly aware of the man handing Sage the torch and picking him up.

"What he needs now is rest," the man said. "I'm so glad you three have finally come! We've been waiting nearly a week, and I was beginning to wonder if we were in the right place."

Arthur wasn't sure he'd heard correctly. The man couldn't have been waiting for them. How could he have been? Arthur didn't even know where they were. Yet even as the thoughts formed, his eyes closed and darkness came.

"It's no that I be disagreeing with yer plan," Andreal said, "but how do we be fighting shadows and blood? Give me a beast, and I will cut it down. Give me a hundred, and I will enjoy meself. But what use is my ax against shadows?"

"We must learn how to fight them," Jack said. "You were in the City of Shadows. You saw what it was like. I'm beginning to realize this battle isn't against the Assassin's servants. If we can't figure out how to defeat the evil itself, the war is already lost. The Assassin is our true enemy."

"Even if you're right, what does it mean?" Wild asked. "How do we fight the blood?"

"I fought it while I was in the schoolhouse. It wasn't like a battle with a sword, but it was a battle as real as any I've seen."

"What do we know about the darkness so far?" Honi said. "Gratefulness cuts through it like an ax through a twig. Is it possible it's that simple?"

Andreal snorted. "I'd be liking to see you stand against a Shadule with nothing but yer gratefulness."

"Do not worry, my friend," Honi said. "Your ax will still be needed. But I think Jack is onto something. It may not be a physical weapon that destroys our true enemy."

"Nothing can destroy it," Jonty said. "The Masters make us stand in the blood for hours every day. Sometimes we're made to sleep on it. The nightmares ..." He shuddered.

"They are not your Masters anymore," Honi said. "No darkness can resist the light forever."

Jonty groaned. "You're seriously talking about just the four of you attacking the town?"

"No"—Andreal placed his massive hand on Jonty's shoulder—"there do be five of us now!"

"There are hundreds of Slaves and Pawns in Ballylesson, and probably fifty Masters and at least thirty Owners." Jonty's eyes were wide and unblinking. "I'd bet there are almost a thousand all told. Not including the blood. You cannot win! If we don't flee, every one of us will die!"

"Death is merely a new beginning," Honi said. "And though I do not seek it, I will embrace it when the time comes."

Jonty held his head in his hands and began to cry. Jack shared an unbelieving look with Wild. *Everything Jonty says makes me feel dirty.* He shivered at the way the Shadow Army ranked its members. Slaves, Pawns, Masters, Owners. *Why would anyone choose to serve the Assassin?*

A thought struck Jack and he suddenly understood the nature of bullies. He spoke carefully so as not to hurt Jonty's feelings. And he began to formulate a plan.

"Strength and numbers aren't always the most important," he said slowly. "It can help, but I've seen the few defeat the many over and again. The Assassin is a bully, and bullies rule by strength and fear. You should know that more than most, Jonty."

Jonty didn't meet Jack's eyes. He stared into the fire as if lost in dark thoughts.

"Do you remember the one time you didn't win? It was snowing. You tried to bully Arthur and me, but you left without doing anything."

"I remember." Jonty brushed away tears. "I tried to take your coat. I was jealous because I knew your mother had made it for you, and my mother never made me anything."

Jack knew Jonty was embarrassed of his mother. Everyone in Ballylesson used to talk about her. She drank all the time and screamed crazy things at anyone who passed her house.

"That's right," Jack said. "You demanded my coat, but I'd seen yours a few days earlier. It was old and torn. I knew you would try to take my coat eventually, so I asked my mother to make another. When you demanded mine, I offered you a brand-new coat made just for you."

Jonty nodded. "I've thought about that day many times. It may be the reason I'm here now. It was the nicest thing anyone has ever done for me." Jonty scrubbed at fresh tears. "But what does that have to do with attacking Ballylesson?"

"After I gave you the coat, you stopped bullying everyone. Eventually you started again, but you were never quite as mean as before."

Jonty lowered his head. "I'm sorry. I was jealous, and you have every right to hate me."

"I don't hate you. I never did. I feared you, but that's different. I think all bullies are the same. Give them what they don't expect, and they don't know what to do. This battle isn't about strength and numbers. It's about something else altogether."

"So you want to offer a Shadule your coat?" Wild asked.

Jack laughed. "No, but I may have an idea of how we can win this fight."

Chapter 15

THE STAR CHILD

Alexia sat high atop a roof in the City of Shadows. The roof was a gaudy thing with silver-plated shingles, a diamond-studded chimney and walls of gold. She surveyed the devastation from the battle that had ended earlier. By her estimation, nearly one-quarter of the city had been destroyed.

She tried not to inhale the stench. Beneath the gold plating that covered the city, something was festering. *No matter how many gems you throw on a dung heap, it's still a dung heap.* She wanted to cover her nose, yet she knew it wouldn't do any good.

She brought her attention back to what mattered. Just below, the Assassin stood atop a platform in the midst of the rubble. Thousands upon thousands of fierce-looking Shadow Souled surrounded him. They watched their master with fear-filled eyes. Belial kept a hand pressed tightly against the new wound in his side, yet black blood still dripped from between his fingers. The Assassin's diamond skin was glossy beneath the sweat that seeped from his every pore, and madness raged in his flaming eyes.

"You have failed me!" His voice was the sound of a beetle-infested carcass. The Shadow Souled stood in absolute silence. "The Children of Prophecy have stolen the Deceiver's Coffer."

Startled gasps erupted from the army.

The Assassin was pale and grimacing. "You will find them. You will bring me both of the children, and you will bring me the coffer!" A roar erupted from the Shadow Army.

The Assassin pointed into the midst of those gathered before him. "Come," he said. A metallic vapor seeped from the ground as the surrounding dark servants shrank back. With the vapor came a thunderous groaning.

"COME!" the Assassin roared. The nearby torches flickered and dimmed as the vapor coalesced into the shape of a dripping monster. Its skin was rippling black metal, and a number of eyes ringed its skull.

"The Odius," Alexia whispered. The creature had taken many forms at the circus, but its true form was frightening beyond words. The Odius raised its gruesome head and howled at the moon.

"Odius, the shadow god, will lead this hunt," the Assassin said. His army was utterly still, and every face was filled with terror. "For every hour the Children of Prophecy remain alive and the Deceiver's Coffer is not in my possession, for every hour I am made to wait, you will be punished." The Assassin spoke to the Odius. "You will consume ten of my followers every hour until your return." The Assassin's eyes flamed brightly.

The dark servants shrank back like wounded dogs. Even the Odius watched its master cautiously.

"In this hunt you will carry only your weapons. You will not eat or sleep until the hunt is over. Only the strongest will survive in my army." The Assassin threw his arms high. "Go! And do not fail me."

Alexia's stomach churned. *He's forcing them to starve until they catch us? No wonder we couldn't lose them; their terror kept them going.*

The Odius raised its head and howled again, its rippling skin contorting into the shape of a winged wolf. It leaped into the air and disappeared into the night. Ten thousand Shadow Souled rose to follow the creature. Some flew; others rode atop winged beasts. For a moment the sky was black.

Once the dark army was gone, the Assassin turned to the dark servants still lining the streets. "Burn the dead and kill every prisoner. The Last Battle has begun, and there will be no mercy."

The hordes shrieked in delight, dancing amid the rubble.

"No!" Alexia whispered. If she'd known the prisoners would be killed after she escaped, she never would have left! *Then I'd have died too,* she thought, *and I'd never have been able to come back to save them.*

The Assassin stepped onto a small, gaudy throne and sat. More than a hundred creatures hoisted the throne onto their shoulders. "Go," the Assassin snarled. As one, the creatures stepped forward, carrying him toward the palace.

Alexia let out a relieved breath. She needed the Assassin to be away if her plan had any hope of succeeding. The low-hanging sun cast long shadows, making it hard to see clearly in a city of slithering darkness. *There!* She spotted Benaiah waiting just inside the arena. A moment later she found Adeline, Summer, and Parker standing in the midst of the gathered throngs. Parker had a very large crate strapped to his back, and all wore the soiled black-and-silver cloaks of the Shadow Souled.

Alexia decided she couldn't wait any longer. *They're going down to kill the prisoners.* She stood and waved to Benaiah. He immediately turned to signal the prisoners waiting in the corridors behind him. Next she signaled Parker, who took the crate from his back and placed it on the ground. Adeline and Summer kept watch, but none of the surrounding dark servants seemed to care what they were doing. Parker knelt by the cage as Alexia reached into her cloak and grabbed a small clump of wax.

Josiah and Juno were already at the palace searching for her mother, and Alexia wanted to join them as soon as possible. But she wouldn't leave until she was sure her plan was working. Parker stood beside the crate and nodded.

She'd once heard Aias say even the best-laid plans lasted barely a minute before a new one had to be made. *This is the only plan I've got,* she thought. *If it doesn't work, we're all dead.* Alexia climbed atop the chimney. She took a deep breath. "Shadow Souled!" she screamed. Every eye turned upward to stare at the girl in the crimson cloak. "It is good to see you again." She curtsied. "I am Alexia Dreager, one of the Children of Prophecy. I will give you one chance to lay down your arms and surrender. Do it now, and I promise mercy—"

"It's the girl!" The dark servants squinted up at her.

"We must kill her!" one snarled.

"The master will give us a great reward!" a creature shrieked.

The dark army surged forward. Alexia broke the chunk of wax in two, then pressed it deep into both ears. Her eyes stayed glued to Parker, who opened the steel crate, then stepped away.

Nothing happened. "Oh no!" she breathed. Her entire plan hinged on what she'd heard after the Myzerahl attack outside London. Arthur Greaves had asked Mrs. Dumphry about the dark servants. She had said, *"Dark servants never travel with the bird for they, too, would be caught in its song. They send it ahead and follow far behind."*

The Shadow Souled surged past Parker, Summer, and Adeline but didn't seem to notice the three children. Every rage-filled eye was focused on Alexia. They swarmed the five-story building faster than Alexia had imagined possible. Then Parker kicked the metal crate. The twenty birds they'd captured finally began to flutter out. "Please let it be enough," she whispered.

The small birds flitted into the air, and though Alexia couldn't hear, she could see the effect of their song. The animals seemed unaffected, but humans screamed in wide-eyed terror at something only they could see. And as they ran from or battled their fears, the beasts were brought down. The dark servants began turning on each other.

Alexia watched the madness in absolute silence. From her perch she saw thousands of prisoners fleeing the coliseum with Benaiah leading the way. The plan was simple: the prisoners would escape while the dark servants were entranced by the Myzerahls' song. So long as the Awakened kept the wax in their ears, they would be safe.

But as the Clear Eyes flooded from a separate entrance of the arena, they didn't stay together like the humans, and they didn't flee. They rounded on the shrieking dark servants. They hated the Assassin, and now that they were free, they would stay and fight, even if it meant every one of them would die.

"No!" Alexia screamed. "You must flee!" She waved her arms frantically. The Awakened escaped with Benaiah as the Clear Eyes attacked. They leaped into the fray, biting, kicking, and clawing everything in their path.

Alexia wanted to cry. Then the words from Mrs. Dumphry's letter sprang to her mind. *"You don't utilize your Soulprint through control; you activate it by surrendering to it. It is not something you do but something you allow to be done through you."* The wind picked up as she watched the madness below. Alexia unclenched her fists and exhaled a long, slow breath as tension melted from her shoulders. She closed her eyes … and surrendered.

The wind grew stronger, whipping into a gale. When she opened her eyes again, a feeling of peace washed over her. She dropped her arms, and the wind exploded away. As one, the Clear Eyes turned to stare at her.

Thousands of visions entered her mind, and Alexia saw herself from the eyes of the animals below. She stood atop the chimney and blazed like the sun. *"STAR CHILD!"* The thought exploded in her mind in a resounding chorus. The image of the constellation that contained Alexia's star, the Lion's Eye, formed in her mind. *"THE STAR CHILD HAS COME. THE FINAL HUNT BEGINS!"*

Alexia shuddered as she was bombarded with the thoughts, images, smells, and vibrations of the Clear Eyes below. For a moment she lost herself; it was all happening too quickly. *Surrender.* She unclenched

her fists and loosened her jaw. In the space of a heartbeat, her Soulprint
solidified. When she responded, it was as natural as breathing.

I am the Star Child whom the ancient ones spoke of. Now that
she was inside the animals' minds, she understood everything. Alexia
wasn't just the Child of Prophecy the Awakened had been seeking;
she was the Star Child, and the Clear Eyes had been searching for her
for thousands of years.

Alexia began to laugh. Her lion friends, Beast and Killer, and the
elephant Ollie had been Clear Eyes. They had been some of her many
protectors. They'd kept her safe from the Assassin and his minions. Yet
until this moment, until she had fully embraced her Soulprint, none
of the Clear Eyes had been sure that she was the Star Child they were
waiting for. Not until she understood her role in this story did she
truly become Star Child.

"We will run together in the Final Hunt." Alexia formed the words
in her mind and then sent them out in a series of images, smells, and
vibrations. *"But it cannot be now, and it cannot be here. Join the Bright
Ones and flee this city. I will come soon."* Bright Ones was what the Clear
Eyes called the Awakened.

*"THE FINAL HUNT COMES! WE WILL JOIN WITH THE
BRIGHT ONES, AND WE WILL RUN TOGETHER AS OUR
ANCESTORS DID IN THE ANCIENT DAYS!"* The Clear Eyes
turned and galloped, ran, slithered, and flew in the direction Benaiah
and the rest of the prisoners had gone.

Alexia's conversation with the animals had lasted only a moment,
and though she still couldn't hear anything, it was obvious the
Myzerahls' song was nearing its finish. In the streets below, dark servants were on their knees begging for mercy from the visions the birds
had woven for them.

The Assassin strode into the madness, fire raging in his eyes. *Please let him be too late to stop the escaping prisoners.* Alexia didn't wait to see what he did. She ran in the direction of the palace. If she was lucky, she'd bought enough time to search the throne room and find her mother. Maybe Josiah and Juno had already found her!

Chapter 16

THE TALE OF TWO JACKS

Jack Staples chuckled to himself as he walked through the woods. The idea had come to him just a few hours earlier, but he hadn't told a soul. He thought it would be far more fun to surprise them. He crept closer, spying on his friends from behind a tree.

"What are we waiting for?" Wild asked. "I thought you said we'd attack at sundown."

The Jack from a few hours earlier smiled. "We're waiting on someone. He should be here any minute now. We'll go once he arrives."

"Who?" Honi asked. "What aren't you telling us, Jack?"

"He's telling you he might have changed the plan a little," Jack said as he stepped out from behind the tree. Wild and Andreal spun, brandishing weapons, then almost dropping them. Jonty darted behind the other Jack.

The Jack from a few hours earlier walked over and extended a hand. "It's good to see you."

"You, too!" Jack said as he shook his own hand. "You're looking well."

Both Jacks turned their attention to the others, who watched in perplexed silence. The Jacks began to laugh.

"I'm sorry I didn't tell you." Jack grinned. "But we needed help, and it was the only way I could think to get it! So I had us wait a few hours, and then I came back in time. Now I can help you fight off the Shadow Souled even while I battle the Assassin's blood."

"It wasn't just your idea," the Jack from the past retorted. "I helped!"

Jack grinned. The younger Jack was clearly as amused as he was.

Honi shook his head. "And have either of you thought through the ramifications of what will happen to the Jack from now in another four hours?"

"What do you mean?" the Jacks said in unison.

"You are changing things from the future," Honi said. "It's one thing to go back and change things once you already know what happened, but now you're changing them before they happen. What if either of you gets injured or dies in this battle?"

Jack's amusement melted. "I hadn't thought about any of that."

"Me, either," said the Jack from a few hours earlier.

"There's nothing to be done about it now, I suppose," Honi said. "Shall we go?"

"You still want to go?" Jack said.

"Yeah, maybe it was a bad idea," the other Jack said.

"Oh, I don't know about that," Honi replied. "I think it has merit. I was just wondering if you had thought it through beyond the ramifications of giving us all a scare. In truth, I think it may be a brilliant plan. Having two of you to help fight this battle may be our only hope of success. You never cease to amaze, Jack Staples." His eyes took in both Jacks. "Neither of you do." He chuckled.

The band of Awakened walked toward the town, with Jonty scurrying along behind them. "Please, you have to see that there's no way to stand against them. We need to run!"

"Jonty Dobson"—Honi stopped—"you are no longer one of the Shadow Souled. You are a member of the Awakened, and I believe in you. Now stop this whining and embrace who you truly are."

"I believe in you," Wild said.

"You can do this, Jonty," the younger Jack encouraged.

"You be my brother now," Andreal said. "And I will be dying for ye if I must."

The words had a physical effect on Jonty. The schoolyard bully stood taller, and his eyes were less haunted than before. Jack didn't wait to see what happened next. As the Jack from the past and his friends entered Ballylesson, he ran into the woods to find a safe place to watch.

Jack walked boldly into the center of town with Honi, Andreal, Wild, and Jonty following just behind. He was no longer amused at the thought of his future self watching from the woods. *What happens to me if he dies?*

None of the Awakened had bothered to dirty their faces or deaden their eyes. They weren't trying to hide. This was Jack's town, his and Wild's. He glanced at Fitzpatrick's Dry Goods Store. His mother had visited the store almost every time she came to town.

Mrs. Walsh's Sweet Shop was covered in shadowed blood, and every window had been smashed. Jack and Arthur used to visit the store once a week, and it was commonly known that Mrs. Walsh had the best toffee in all Ireland. His anger grew as he walked. *How could they do this to my home?*

He turned to face O'flannigans and stopped. The Shadule lurking inside was bent bonelessly over a table, studying a map. A part of Jack couldn't believe what he was doing, but another part didn't care. He'd spent much of the past year trying to fix things that were unfixable. He'd spent most of his time running from who he was meant to be. In this moment, in this place, he would fully embrace his role in this world of light and darkness. *No more running.*

"Shadule!" Jack was happy his voice didn't waver. With all the adrenaline coursing through him, he was surprised his entire body wasn't shaking. The Shadule peered outside. "I hope I'm not interrupting things, but I think you and I should have a chat."

The Shadule moved fluidly through the broken picture window out onto the street. "Who are you, boy?" it rasped.

"My name is Jack Staples. And I am one of the Children of Prophecy."

The Shadule hissed. Another five Shadow Souled stepped out of O'flannigans as more gathered in the street.

"But more than that, I am a citizen of this town, and I am here to tell you to leave Ballylesson. Leave now, and no harm will come to you."

The Shadule turned its milky-white eyes on Jack's friends. When its gaze fell on Jonty, it let out a gurgling laugh.

"This? This is your army?" Its body stretched to add a pace to its height. "Three Awakened and a slave who belongs me!" The creature's laughter made Jack's skin crawl. "Come here, slave!" The Shadule pointed at Jonty. "Prostrate yourself before me or die."

"P-please," Jonty whimpered. "Please can we go? We shouldn't be here! I told you we couldn't win!"

"Jonty Dobson does not belong to you," Jack said. "He never did. He is one of the Awakened, and he is my friend. If you want him, you'll have to go through me."

By now, more than a hundred dark servants had gathered in the street. Jack and his friends formed a circle as Jack drew Ashandar and held it high. "I claim this town for the Awakened! And I offer mercy to every dark servant here. You joined the Assassin's army because you were offered power and glory. Yet you have become his slaves. Look at Jonty Dobson!" Jack turned and pointed at Jonty. "He is free. If *you* want to be free, join us. I offer forgiveness for your crimes and a life of purpose."

For a long moment, nothing happened. Jack could see many of the dark servants thinking through what he'd said. But then the moment was gone. "Take them," the Shadule rasped.

There was no more time for conversation.

Alexia didn't look down as she climbed the Assassin's palace. It was fifty stories high, but thanks to her Soulprint, it took only a few minutes to reach the top. She climbed onto the throne-room balcony and spotted Juno and Josiah poking about near one of the mammoth pillars.

"I take it you haven't found anything yet?" she said as she entered.

Both children spun with weapons raised.

"Did you climb up here?" Juno lowered her whip and looped it back onto her belt.

Josiah shouldered his quarterstaff. "What happened out there? Did they get away?"

Alexia looked back toward the arena. "I don't know where they are now, but they were well on their way before I left. We don't have much time, though. The Assassin is dealing with the Myzerahls, but he'll be coming back soon."

"We've been looking for trapdoors or hidden levers," Juno said, "but this place is so big that a secret chamber could be anywhere."

Alexia nodded as her eyes scanned the walls and floor. Standing between the balcony and the throne was a colossal, golden statue of the Assassin. It was a hideous thing that stood with palms facing upward and was so large, its head disappeared into the vaulted ceiling. Only its flaming eyes were visible.

Alexia walked to the center of the chamber and stood at the base of the throne. It was as large as a house and encrusted in diamonds and gemstones. She searched for a latch or lever as she climbed the stairs to the throne.

When she reached the top, Alexia sat down and scanned the throne room. *Mother has to be here!* Her anxiety rose with each passing second. Josiah and Juno searched around another pillar as Alexia leaned heavily on the throne's armrests.

She wrinkled her nose. The entire city reeked of death, but the foulness seemed to be strongest here. She grabbed the armrests and leaned forward. *Mrs. Dumphry's letter said my mother was here. Could she have been mistaken?* Alexia searched for anything that might be out of place. She slammed a fist into the armrest in frustration. *If we don't find her soon, the Assassin will come and—* Both armrests sank downward.

Alexia's breath caught as the gold on the seat beneath her began to ripple. Her eyes followed the ripple as it spread down the throne. It hit the floor with a golden splash, then flowed outward. It was as if someone had thrown a stone into a lake; except rather than fading, the ripple became larger the farther it went.

"I think I found something," Alexia said slowly. The golden ripple grew into a wave. "Oh no!" she shouted. "Run!"

Josiah and Juno had already seen the growing wave. They sprinted toward the statue of the Assassin, but the wave was on their heels. Juno reached it first and began to climb, but Josiah was too late. The wave of gold carried him upward, and Josiah leaped from its crest, grabbing Juno's hand. Alexia sighed as Juno pulled Josiah to safety.

The golden wave crashed into the wall, then flowed upward. When it hit the ceiling, it continued to grow, flowing inward. Alexia ducked low as the wave collided with itself directly above the throne, thrashing like churned water before it dissipated.

Alexia gaped at the transformed throne room. The gaudy illusion was gone. It had become a chamber of horrors.

Spikes, razors, spears, and halberds protruded from wall, floor, and ceiling. Piled beneath the spiked floor was something splintered and pale. "It's bones," Josiah said in a strangled voice.

Alexia's stomach churned. Between the skewers, the ground was covered in bones. Many were broken and splintered beyond recognition; many were not. Alexia shuddered. The throne—it was made entirely of bones.

The floor was so covered in razors that it would be impossible to move without being cut to ribbons.

"So what now?" Josiah called. "This isn't a prison; it's a death chamber."

"Alexia!" Juno gasped. Her eyes were locked on the ceiling. "Look!"

A woman was hanging from the barbed ceiling. She was filthy, and her clothes ragged, but even so, Alexia recognized her.

"Mother!" she cried. "Mother, it's me! Wake up! We've come to rescue you!" But her mother did not stir.

Chapter 17

AN IMPROBABLE HAPPENING

Jack watched from the safety of the woods as the dark servants rushed in. Yet for every enemy that attacked, one more stayed back. The offer of mercy from the other Jack had obviously gotten their attention. Even so, the five Awakened were hopelessly outnumbered.

Jack's muscles began to cramp as he watched the younger Jack fight. He fought with a master's grace as Ashandar guided his every move. *I'm feeling his tiredness!* Jack realized. *Whatever happens to him happens to me.* The thought scared him. If the Jack from the past died in battle … He decided not to think about it. He'd wasted enough time already. *All right*, he thought, *this better work!*

Jack closed his eyes and embraced his note. It was no longer hard to hear the ring of Time; it was part of him. He flew backward, leaving the safety of the woods to appear in the center of the street barely a block away from the battle. His feet sank into the webbed darkness until he was calf-deep in the Assassin's blood.

He'd traveled to the heart of it, to the spot where the Assassin's blood had first fallen. The blood attacked with a fury. Webbing clung to his legs and lurched upward. Anger and jealousy welled inside him.

How could I call Jonty my friend? The boy had bullied him for years. That wasn't something you just forgave. He needed to make Jonty pay. He was Jack Staples, the Child of Prophecy! *I'll show him exactly how it felt! I'll do to him what he did to me.*

"No!" Jack said through gritted teeth. "Revenge is not justice. It was right to forgive Jonty."

The darkness shrieked and redoubled its attack, slithering over his shoulders and up his neck. Jack struggled to breathe as shadowed webs slipped into his mouth and down his throat. Still Jack stood his ground. The black blood ripped at his clothes and tore at his skin. Shadowed barbs pierced his eyes, but he refused to scream.

Rage, bitterness, envy, greed, regret, and pride were a cauldron in his chest, yet Jack fought them with all his heart. The web of blood buried him in a misery beyond anything he'd imagined. It tore at his soul. Physical pain was nothing to what he was feeling now. He locked his knees and pressed his lips together. *I will not scream. I will not give in!*

Jack Staples battled three Oriax and a strange penguin-like creature at the same time. He was careful not to step too far forward for fear of breaking the circle. All five Awakened stood back to back, and though they were terribly outnumbered, so long as the enemy didn't separate them, they could survive awhile.

Jack saw himself from the corner of his eye. The Jack from the future stood beneath a mountain of raging darkness. Jack and his four friends were merely a decoy. They were to keep the Shadow Souled busy while the future Jack fought the true battle. While Jack was distracted, the penguin pierced his shoulder, but he kicked it away.

Beside Jack, Andreal swung his axes in a deadly maelstrom, cleaving through dark servants like a razor through leather. The giant laughed as he worked his axes. He seemed to enjoy the act of destroying his enemy. Honi stood on Jack's other side and moved with a serpent's grace. The old man used his knobby walking stick like a quarterstaff; each time it struck one of the Shadow Souled, golden sparks exploded from both ends and the enemy fell. Jonty and Wild fought behind him, obscured from view, but he could hear them working their weapons.

Jack glanced quickly at the other Jack, who was almost lost to sight as he stood beneath an ever-growing mountain of the Assassin's blood. Almost all of the dark webbing that covered the town had slithered back to gather in one place, crawling atop itself as it attempted to crush the future Jack.

Jack screamed as a deep gash appeared on his shoulder. He saw the Jack from the past kick a birdlike creature away. He ignored the pain; he needed every ounce of energy if he was to stand against the torrent of hatred and misery. The mountain of blood grew ever larger. This is what he had hoped for. He needed to draw every last drop of the Assassin's blood into one place.

Dark wind tore at Jack as hate-filled barbs pierced his skin. Hundreds of emotions raged inside him, but for each one he tried to offer the opposite response. For anger he offered forgiveness; for cynicism, faith. A wave of depression rolled over him, and he searched for a joy-filled memory.

Voices erupted from within the gale. "IT WAS YOUR FAULT YOUR MOTHER DIED," they screamed.

Unbearable guilt weighed down on him, but Jack remembered the look on his mother's face as she saved his life. *"Ah, my Jack. Not even death can keep me from my children. Now, don't come back here again. You cannot save me. I will always love you."* He embraced the memory and shouted at the wind, "My mother loved me enough to give her life so I might live!"

The darkness shrieked and sank into Jack's bones. Outside the mountain, the band of Awakened fought the Shadow Souled. *What kind of despicable person could follow the Assassin?* The moment the thought formed, the mountain of blood thickened.

The Shadow Souled are the reason for so much of the pain in the world. He wanted to kill them all. The weight of the mountain became unbearable, and Jack crumbled to his knees, but he didn't care; his anger felt justified. *Of course it's right to hate the Shadow Souled!*

A voice pierced the growing darkness. It was still and small and came from somewhere deep inside his heart. *"No. The dark servants have been tricked into serving the Assassin. It is not right to hate them!"*

Jack lunged upward so he was standing once again. "No!" he shouted as he raised his arms. "I don't hate them!" He thought of Jonty Dobson. The poor boy had grown up with brothers who were cruel and a mother who was far crueler. Yes, the dark servants were fighting for the wrong side, but they were not his enemy. They were his brothers and sisters, and he loved them.

The darkness shrieked, the shadowed barbs suddenly finding no purchase.

"There are three things you must always remember," Mrs. Dumphry had written. *"Three things that will guide you—forgiveness, mercy, and most of all, love."* It was the only clear thought he had. Amid the misery and depression, the rage and self-pity; amid the crushing sadness, Jack heard it again.

"LOVE!" This time the voice had come from his heart, and Jack knew who it belonged to. It was the voice of the poet. It was the voice of the Author, and he was speaking to Jack in the midst of the battle.

"YOU ARE NOTHING!" the darkness screamed.

"YOU WILL NEVER BE GREAT," it raged.

"YOU WILL NEVER BE ENOUGH."

"YOU'LL LET EVERYONE DOWN."

"YOUR LIFE IS MEANINGLESS!"

"YOU WERE A MISTAKE!"

"NOBODY LOVES YOU!"

"IT WOULD BE BETTER IF YOU HADN'T BEEN BORN!"

Jack Staples squeezed his eyes shut and shook his head. "I choose love!" he screamed. He raised his arms high and shouted, "I am the Child of Prophecy, and in the name of the Author, I command you to leave!"

The blood howled as Jack placed both hands on Ashandar's hilt and unsheathed the blade, thrusting it into the ground. He collapsed to his knees as the shadows shriveled and dissipated. The dark servants halted their attack on the other Jack and his friends. Every last one stood silently, watching him with awe-filled eyes.

"Impossible!" the Shadule shrieked. "No weapon can stand against the blood of our master!"

"I didn't need a weapon, Shadule," Jack said, drained of energy. "Hear me!" He stood stiffly. "Any dark servant who wishes to join the Awakened may do so now. We don't care what you've done or who you are; we will embrace you as our brothers and sisters. But if you will not forsake the Assassin, then I command you to run. In the name of the Author, leave this town and don't look back."

Throughout the street, hundreds of men, women, and children dropped their weapons. They stood looking at Jack as if unsure what to do next. Others whimpered as they turned and ran blindly away from Ballylesson.

"No!" the Shadule shrieked. "Kill them! I command you to kill the Awakened."

When none of the former dark servants moved, the creature hissed. Its wings unfurled from its body, and it rose into the air. "This is nothing, boy! The Shadow Lord will destroy this world, and your victory will soon be forgotten."

Honi limped forward and thrust his staff into the air. An explosion of colored sparks shot at the Shadule and struck the creature in the chest. Honi sent more colored streaks toward the Shadule until it finally shrieked and disappeared into the sky.

For a long moment, no one moved. It was Doctor Falvey who finally raised a fist to the air. "All hail our new king, Jack Staples!" he shouted. Before Jack could do anything to stop them, the ragtag group of former dark servants echoed the doctor's response. "All hail the king, Jack Staples!" One by one they dropped to their knees.

Wild wore an amused look as Andreal let out a booming laugh. Jack felt his cheeks grow warm.

"I feel strange," the Jack from the past said. He looked at his hand curiously. "I think we've caught up with the—"

The Jack from the past faded into nothing as the past and present became one.

Chapter 18

FEAR IN THE AIR

Alexia's eyes kept shifting to her mother. She couldn't believe it. Her mother was alive! She was filthy and dressed in rags and looked far older than Alexia remembered, but it was her. She hung facedown, parallel to the ground, with cords wrapped around each limb. She was unconscious, and there was a pale, almost silvery sheen to her skin, but she was breathing.

"You're doing great!" Alexia called to Juno. Her friend had climbed up the distorted statue of the Assassin and was slowly traversing the ceiling.

"Please don't fall, please don't fall, please don't fall," Juno whispered as she moved from one spike to the next. Alexia had wanted to rescue her mother, but even with the help of her Soulprint, it would have been impossible to cross the floor. So it had fallen to Juno or Josiah. Josiah had grudgingly agreed that Juno was the better climber, so off she'd gone.

"Whatever you do, be careful of the—" Alexia's breath caught as Juno slid down a particularly long skewer. She neared the razor-tipped bottom and placed her feet against it, then leaped away and grabbed hold of Alexia's dangling mother. Both women swung back and forth as Juno pulled herself up so she was sitting on Madeleine Dreager's back.

"You did brilliantly," Alexia called. "I don't think I could have done better."

"My Soulprint may not be as strong as yours, but my balance is better than most," Juno said as she climbed up the ropes connected to the ceiling. She reached the top and began unspooling the excess rope. In a matter of seconds, she'd lowered the rope so it was hanging just out of Alexia's reach.

"I don't mean to be the bearer of bad news," Josiah called from his perch on the statue's hand, "but the Assassin is approaching the palace! I think he must have dealt with the Myzer-whatevers already."

Alexia wanted to kick something. They were cutting it close. "We need to do this now," she called up to Juno. "It won't take him long to get here."

"I'm going as fast as I can," Juno called. She'd looped the dangling rope around her leg, then slid back down to Alexia's mother. Juno swung the rope over to Alexia so she could grab hold of it.

"Got it!" Alexia called.

Juno unsheathed a knife from inside her boot. She pulled Madeleine Dreager close and then sliced the ropes binding her to the ceiling.

Alexia's mother dropped into Juno's arms. Juno ever so slowly began to slide down her rope until she hovered just above Alexia.

"Are you ready?" Juno grunted.

"Ready!" Alexia said through clenched teeth.

Juno thrust Madeleine Dreager toward the throne. Alexia let go of the rope and caught her mother as Juno swung outward. Alexia quickly laid her mother on the throne, then turned to reach out a hand. Juno was swinging back toward the throne. Alexia grabbed her hand and pulled her to safety.

"Thank you," Alexia gasped into Juno's ear as she wrapped her in a hug. "Thank you for risking your life to save my mother."

"I'm glad we found her," Juno said. "Far too many of us have lost our mothers."

"I don't mean to interrupt," Josiah called again, "but won't the Assassin be here any minute? Mightn't it be best if we save the hugging for later?"

Alexia quickly tied two loops in the bottom of the rope, where she and Juno could place their feet. She then lifted her mother so she was carrying her like a sack of potatoes.

Alexia's hands shook as both girls placed a foot inside the loops. "Are you ready?" she asked.

"Ready," Juno said.

"One ..." Alexia gripped the rope with one hand and her mother with the other. "Two ..." She took a deep breath. "Three!" The girls stepped from the throne and swung out over the barbs.

They soared past the grotesque statue of the Assassin toward the opening to the balcony. Both girls pushed with their feet to gain momentum. Back past Josiah and the statue of the Assassin and over the throne, then back to the balcony again, each swing going just a little higher and farther. The thin rope creaked and groaned.

Josiah watched the girls swing past again and again. "Are you sure it will hold?" he called.

"We're out of options," Alexia shouted as they swung high above the throne. "This is it. You need to jump!" They swung back past the statue of the Assassin. "Now!"

"Do it!" Juno yelled at the same time.

Josiah leaped from his perch and landed on Juno's back. The rope swung toward the balcony, and all three children screamed as they passed above the gleaming razors and dry bones. As they neared the top of the arc, Juno cut the rope to send them tumbling to the balcony below.

Alexia groaned as she landed flat on her stomach with her mother on her back.

"No!" a voice roared from somewhere inside the throne room.

Alexia froze. The Assassin had come.

"Impossible!" he screamed.

Alexia peeked through a small crack in the balcony. She shuddered at the sight of the Assassin standing at the far end of the chamber. He was hunched over with one hand pressed against the fresh wound in his side. His fiery eyes were fixed on the ceiling, where Madeleine Dreager had been prisoner only minutes earlier. Alexia held her breath as the Assassin scanned the throne room.

Belial had changed in the hours since she'd last seen him. His skin hung limp, and dark sweat poured from him, puddling at his feet. But mostly it was the darkness—waves of doom pulsed from him. The shadowed gloom pulled at her vision, threatening to steal all light from the world. She turned away and leaned against the balcony. She was too afraid to look on the creature any longer.

"I will find you!" The Assassin's voice resounded above them. "I will destroy everything you love. Then I will feast on your souls."

She would have shrieked if she hadn't been too afraid to open her mouth. Impossibly, the Assassin was leaning against the balcony. All he needed to do was look down, and he would see Alexia and her friends. Yet his attention was given to the horizon.

"The end has come, and the prophecy demands it. The Children of Prophecy will die at my hands. And as their light fades, this world will be reformed into my image!"

Alexia didn't move, not even to breathe.

"It is time for the world to see who they truly serve," the Assassin rasped. Then the demon let out a beastly roar as the sound of something ripping filled Alexia's ears. She cracked an eye to see a dark cloud explode from the throne room. It was blacker than any pitch, and as it rocketed across the sky, it swallowed the light of the world. The moon and stars disappeared, and still the darkness spread, ripping across the horizon. The only light to break through the darkness came from Alexia's and Jack's stars.

"The end has come. My final victory is here!"

Alexia trembled at the wheezing voice. It was as if the words came from a mouth unaccustomed to speech. The demon let out a gurgling roar and leaped from the throne room, quickly disappearing into the darkened sky. It was too dark to see clearly, but whatever was flying away was far from human.

From horizon to horizon, the sky was cloaked in shadowed gloom, and Alexia knew it was still spreading. She remembered Elion's words. *"It is the Assassin's Shadow. It is his essence. It is fear and hatred, pride and jealousy. And those who bathe in its darkness must fight to stay pure."*

For a long moment, no one said a word.

"We need to get out of here," Juno whispered. "I don't know what just happened, but I've never been so afraid in my life."

Alexia nodded. She felt it too. The sky radiated fear. Each time she inhaled, she felt dread growing in her chest. "I don't think we have any choice but to climb down," she said. "We'll never be able to cross the throne room."

Josiah crawled to the edge of the balcony and peered over. "Just when I thought it couldn't get any worse," he muttered.

Alexia tied her mother to her back and was first over the ledge. She wanted to show Josiah and Juno where to place their hands and feet. As she began the climb down, Alexia couldn't help smiling. She didn't know what came next. She didn't even know if they'd make it safely out of the city, but at the moment, she didn't care. The Last Battle had begun, and the end of the world might come. But her mother was alive.

Chapter 19

TWO DAYS FROM NOW

"Arthur, you need to wake up. It's time to go."

Arthur heard the voice but didn't care. He hated being woken from a good dream more than anything. In his dream he'd been having dinner with his mother and father. They were sitting around the table laughing. Though he'd only just awoken, the dream was already slipping from his mind. *What were we laughing at?*

"Arthur, I know you're tired, but we need to leave. Something evil is coming," the girl's voice said.

He refused to open his eyes. *Father was telling a story about a pig that wandered into a butcher's shop. And the pig said something.*

"I don't know," the girl said. "We may not have any choice but to carry him."

"Let me find Eric," someone else said.

The butcher was surprised by the pig in his shop ... Arthur scoured the memory. He bolted upright and threw his arms wide. "Then the pig says, 'I just tried some bacon, and I'll take as much as you've got'!" Arthur had to wipe tears of laughter from his eyes.

"No need to get Eric," Sage said slowly. "Though we may have need of a healer."

Arthur couldn't stop chuckling. "The pig wanted to eat bacon ... Don't you get it?"

"I'm afraid not." Sage placed a hand against Arthur's forehead. "And we may not have time to discuss it right now. We let you sleep as long as we could, but something evil is coming, and we need to get ready to defend ourselves."

Arthur sighed as he stood and stretched tired muscles. He could feel the Poet's Coffer in his jacket pocket. The box was warm against his chest, and the longer he carried it, the surer he was that it was changing him somehow. He felt ... bolder. "Mrs. Dumphry once told me that if we couldn't find the time to laugh, we might as well just tell the Assassin he's won. Except when she said it, it sounded smarter than that." Arthur checked the knives at his belt. "All right, then, shall we go see about this evil?"

Sage shook her head. "You're different than you were just a few days ago. Where did you find this sudden burst of confidence?"

Arthur blushed. "I suppose I've grown tired of being afraid all the time. And I'm tired of always being looked after. Seeing as I'm on the Council of Seven, I need to be the one who's looking after others."

"I doubt even Mrs. Dumphry understood what a good choice she made when she gave you her seat. You are wise and you are strong, and I like you very much, Arthur Greaves." Sage leaned in and kissed him on the cheek. "Now, it's past time we leave."

Sage left Arthur with his mouth agape and his hand on his cheek. "What was that?" he whispered.

"That was a kiss, silly!" Aliyah giggled.

Arthur jumped. "I know!" he said quickly. "I've seen a kiss before! I was just surprised, that's all! We'd better be going."

When Arthur stumbled into the light of the setting sun, he saw tens of thousands of Awakened gathered in the valley.

"How many are there?" he whispered.

"More than sixty thousand," Sage said. She turned. "Arthur, this is Eric. He is on the Council of Three that leads this army, and he's the one who insisted they wait here for us."

A tall, shaggy-haired man with wire-rimmed spectacles offered Arthur his hand. "I've heard quite a few stories of the Lightning Dancer, and I'm mighty pleased to meet you, I am!"

Arthur took Eric's hand. "It's good to meet you, too."

"I'm glad we weren't waiting around fer nothing," Eric said. "We've been sittin' in this valley fer a week now, and I'd begun to wonder if we was being foolish, I was."

"I don't understand," Arthur said. "We didn't know we'd be here until we arrived, and I don't even know where here is. How could you have been waiting for us?"

"I didn't know who we were waiting fer," Eric said. "But I was sure we was waiting fer someone. I felt a prompting that we should stay, and thank the Author we did! Seeing as you carry the Poet's Coffer, you'll be needin' an army at yer back."

"What do you mean you felt a prompting?"

"The prompting of the Author," Eric said as if it were the most obvious thing in the world.

Arthur looked at Sage, his eyebrows raised.

"For all your wisdom, I forget that your scales have only recently fallen off," she said. "Have you ever had a feeling you couldn't shake? Or maybe you thought you needed to do something or say something that didn't make sense—except you just couldn't get rid of the feeling?"

"Yes," Arthur said.

"This is one of the many ways the Author speaks to us. The more we learn to listen to the Author's voice, the clearer it becomes."

Arthur turned back to Eric. "So you kept an army of sixty thousand Awakened camped here because of a feeling?"

"Thirty-one thousand Lambs, eleven thousand Healers, six thousand Shepherds, five thousand Craftsmen, three thousand Mentors, two thousand Artists, and one thousand, two hundred and forty Poets, to be exact." Eric bowed his head. "And, yes, we were sure the Author was speaking, and though we couldn't make sense of it, we weren't going to move until he was moving us."

"Lambs, Healers, and … what were the others?"

Sage smiled. "The Awakened have ranks just like any army. When your scales first fall off, you are a Lamb. With a little training, you become a Healer, Shepherd, Craftsman, Artist, Mentor, or Poet."

Arthur's scales had fallen off nearly a year ago, and this was the first he'd heard of it. "So what does that make me?"

Aliyah chuckled from the tent entrance. "From the stories I've heard, you dance when you fight. I'd say that makes you an Artist."

Arthur nodded. "I like the sound of that!" He turned back to Eric. "What's this I hear about something evil coming?"

"It's me Soulprint. It tells me where the enemy is, it does! Right now it tells me something of the purest evil is coming from the south." Eric turned southward. "And whatever it is, it's sure comin' fast. It'll be here any minute now."

Arthur's eyes scanned the southern horizon. "If you're right, shouldn't we be able to see it?"

"Like I said, it be moving fast. But the Poet's Coffer is drawin' the Shadow Souled like Clear Eyes to an Oasis. Dark armies are coming from almost every direction. Though the closest is more than a day away."

"We need to get the Awakened moving," Arthur said, "and we need to go south. Mr. Staples told me to get the coffer to the Valley of Elah. He said it was four days' march from the Quagmire. He said that's where we'll find Jack and Alexia."

A scream sounded from somewhere in the valley. Arthur turned as many more screams erupted from the army of the Awakened. All eyes faced southward. A vast, slithering darkness rocketed across the sky, stretching the length of the horizon.

"What is it?" Sage gripped Arthur's hand.

"I lived through this day once before," Arthur said. "Elion called it the Assassin's Shadow, though she didn't know how he made it." The darkness swept over them and continued past, blanketing the world. "About this time tomorrow, we will have caught up with the present."

Arthur turned to Eric. "I need to talk to the army. Is there a way to do it so that everyone can hear me?"

Eric tore his eyes from the slithering darkness. "You can use a Whispering Stone if ye like," he said as he picked up a stone from the ground and studied it a moment. "This should do the trick." He handed Arthur the stone.

Arthur glanced at Sage, wondering if Eric might not be fully sane.

"Say what you need to say." Sage smiled at him. "They will hear you."

When he coughed to clear his throat, the sound echoed across the valley. Sage watched with an amused look but didn't say a word. "My name is Arthur Greaves," his voice boomed. "And I sit on the Council of Seven, as does Sage." Arthur realized he didn't know her family name and blushed. "You must not fear the dark cloud. There is no darkness so great that the light cannot chase it away. We are the Awakened. We carry the light of the Author inside us. His blood flows in our veins. So do not give in to fear or worry. And do not lose heart. We will defeat this darkness!"

The army of Awakened threw their arms high and cheered. When he saw Sage grinning at him, Arthur stepped back, feeling suddenly foolish. "What's so funny?"

"You told us you wouldn't be a good Council member," Sage said, "but I don't think I've ever seen such a natural leader."

Arthur was almost thankful for the Assassin's Shadow. Maybe Sage wouldn't be able to see how red his cheeks had become.

"Arthur Reginald Alexander Greaves, you come here right this instant!"

Arthur gasped. His mother and father were stalking up the valley. A broadsword twice as long as Arthur was slung across his father's back, and his mother carried two knitting needles and some yarn.

"Mother! Father!" Arthur shouted as he ran down the valley and leaped into his father's arms. "What are you doing here?"

"I could ask the same of you," his father said. "We've spent most of this past year searching for you. I can barely believe it!"

"Oh, how we missed you," his mother whispered. "Now what's this about the Council of Seven? You're far too old to have your mouth washed out with soap for telling tales, but you really ought to know better!"

Arthur began to laugh. Soon his mother and father joined in. Before long they were laughing so hard they were crying.

"Can you please tell everyone to stop bowing all the time? It's embarrassing!" Jack donned another jacket. An hour earlier it had been sweltering hot, and now it was snowing outside.

"Yes, my king. I'll do it right away." Wild chuckled and bowed low.

"It's not funny," Jack protested. "If someone sees you do it, they'll never stop."

"Why else do you think I'm doing it?" Wild said. "There's not been much to laugh at lately, and Jack Staples turned king of the Awakened, is one of the funniest things I've ever heard."

Jack rolled his eyes.

"It do be funny," Andreal said. The giant knelt beside the fireplace, working a flint and stone. A series of sparks flew out as a small flame formed.

"Jack"—Honi wrapped a fresh bandage around his wounded leg as he spoke—"though the Awakened have no need of a king, these former Shadow Souled seem to need one. In time they will come to understand our ways, but it may be easier for them if they have someone they can follow. The Last Battle has come, and we don't have the time to train them properly. At the best of times, it takes months for someone to understand what it means to be Awakened. If it's easier for them to think of you as their king, I say let them."

Jack shook his head. He couldn't go anywhere without people bowing. To make things worse, the Assassin's Shadow had come and blotted out the sky. Even without looking at it, Jack could feel the effects of the dark cloud. *We rid Ballylesson of his blood, and then the Assassin's Shadow comes.* His shiver had little to do with the cold.

They were in Jack's family home—Wild and Honi and Andreal, who lay stretched out before the fire. Jonty Dobson stood near the entry with his eyes glued to Jack. He seemed to think of himself as Jack's personal bodyguard. Though Jack wished Jonty would find someone else to cling to, he didn't have the heart to tell him so. Jonty had no friends, and all of his family had chosen to follow the Assassin.

"I wish I knew why Mrs. Dumphry needed this." Jack ran his fingers over the small tin in his hands. When he'd opened it, he'd been surprised to find a handful of leaves and spices.

"I never told you what happened the day my scales fell off," Wild said.

"No," Jack said. He remembered the day well. Wild had dropped to the schoolhouse floor and started screaming about his eyes. "We all thought you'd gone mad. And then you were sent off to the asylum, or at least that's what we were told."

"Mrs. Dumphry let that story spread so no one would ask questions. The truth is, my scales fell off because of what you are holding in your hands."

"What do you mean?"

"My Soulprint is different from most. I can't summon lightning or run up walls or travel in time. What I do is far subtler. I know when someone is hiding something, as well as where they are hiding it. And if you've lost something, I can tell you exactly where it is."

"I thought your Soulprint had something to do with the bow and quarterstaff."

"No, I'm good with the weapons because I train hard." Wild grinned. "On the day my scales fell off, I used my Soulprint without meaning to. I think it's why my scales fell off. I didn't know what I was looking for, but I was sure Mrs. Dumphry had hidden something in the floorboards beneath her desk. And when she went out into the schoolyard, I found it. When I saw it, my scales fell off, and by the end of the day, Mrs. Dumphry had sent me to train in Agartha."

"But what *is* it?" Jack studied the leaves and spices.

"I have no idea," Wild said, "but it's important to Mrs. Dumphry."

Jack glanced out the window at the slithering sky. He could feel misery radiating down. "We've done what we came here for," he said. "And we've almost caught up with the present. Before she left us in the Great Oasis, Elion told Alexia and me that the end was near. She said the world couldn't survive beneath the Assassin's Shadow for more than a few days. So I suppose we'd better get to this valley Mrs. Dumphry wrote about."

"The Valley of Elah is on the other side of the world," Honi said as he blew a smoke ring from his pipe. "If we leave today, we could reach it in six months, maybe less."

Jack whistled. "Could we use a World Portal?"

"Perhaps," Honi replied, "but every portal I know of is in the hands of the Shadow Souled. We would have to fight our way in."

"Jack, what be the chance of taking us there with yer Soulprint?" Andreal said. "Could ye no carry us the same way ye did when we went back to the circus?"

"No." Jack shook his head. "It's too dangerous. You saw what happened last time. I almost killed everyone."

"It wasn't your fault the circle broke," Wild said. "It was Alexia's."

"What do you mean?"

"She twisted her hands around so she could slip away. I watched her do it. I don't know why, but I think she decided she didn't want to come back with us."

Jack was still sure it was his fault. He'd just told Alexia she was his sister, and she'd been furious with him for not telling her sooner.

"Either way, it's too dangerous." Jack shook his head. "There are hundreds of Awakened here. If even one of them breaks the chain—"

"You don't need to take everyone," Honi said. "The whole world is fighting to survive. The Last Battle isn't happening in just one place. There will be battles in every country, city, and town. But you need to be in the valley, and I for one plan to stand by your side."

"As do I," said Wild.

"If ye try to leave me behind, I'll break both yer legs!" Andreal said cheerfully.

Jonty Dobson stepped forward. "I will die for you if I must."

Jack met each of his friends' eyes. "Thank you," he said. "Your friendships mean the world to me." He turned to Jonty and placed his hand on the boy's shoulders. "I need someone here I can trust. You heard Honi. There will be many more battles in the days to come, and someone needs to lead *these* people. You are the only one who knows what they've been through."

"You really think I can?"

"I'm sure of it. Just remember that the Awakened do not lead through strength of arm but through strength of character."

Tears wet Jonty's cheeks. "You're my very best friend." He sniffled. "I promise I won't let you down!"

Chapter 20

THE VALLEY OF ELAH

"Are you sure this is where they're meant to be?" Josiah said in a hushed voice.

"It looks pretty deserted to me," Juno whispered.

Alexia carefully laid her mother on the street as she studied the building. "This is where I told them to go. I—"

"It took you long enough!" a voice called from the shadows.

Alexia saw Benaiah strutting out of the adjacent building. His arms were spread wide, and he looked truly happy.

Josiah let out a relieved sigh.

"Your plan was good," Benaiah said to Alexia. "I sent everyone through the World Portal. Summer and Addy didn't like leaving without you, but someone needed to lead. It took forever to get everyone through, but the last group just left. They're waiting for us in the Valley of Elah."

"They made it? The Awakened and the Clear Eyes are safely away from here?" Alexia had only half believed the plan would work.

"Three thousand, four hundred, and thirty-two Awakened, and somewhere over seven thousand Clear Eyes. It was crazy. Lion and lamb, bear and warthog stood side by side without so much as growling at one another."

Alexia wrapped him in a hug. "You did brilliantly. Thank you, Benaiah."

"Thank you for coming back for us," he whispered. "Now, can we get out of here, please?"

Jack's eyes lingered on his hometown.

"Do you think we'll ever come back?" Wild asked.

"I don't know," Jack said. "But I hope so." He squinted into the town square. Jonty and a number of others had gathered around something. "What are they doing?" he asked. They were all looking at something on the ground. A moment later a post was raised, and flapping at the top was a white flag with the head of a golden, roaring lion. "What is that?"

Honi and Andreal laughed.

"It's a surprise they made for you," Wild said. "As the newly crowned king of the Awakened, they wanted you to have your own flag."

"Mrs. Dumphry will have my head. She'll think I've become full of myself." The crowd gathered around the flag, and all eyes turned to Jack. After a moment he shook his head irritably and raised his arms. A triumphant cheer rose from the townsfolk. The flag made him feel the fool, but if it helped give them courage … He glanced at the slithering sky and shivered. *They're going to need all the hope they can muster.*

"You all know what happened last time I tried this," Jack said. "I need you to hold on tight, and no matter what happens, don't let go." He glanced upward. Somewhere high above the Assassin's Shadow, night had fallen, yet Jack and Alexia's stars had grown brighter. They were the only light that pierced the slithering darkness. Jack glanced at his hometown one last time before he embraced his note and the group rocketed from the hilltop, flying backward through the air.

Jack smiled as they soared—it felt so natural to use his Soulprint now. The group began to drop, and he looked down to see that they were arriving in the midst of a battle. Even as his feet touched the ground, he unsheathed Ashandar and pivoted forward to strike an Oriax about to sink its teeth into an older man who'd fallen. Jack pulled the man to his feet, then spun around to stave off another attacking Oriax.

"What's happening here?" Jack asked.

"I only just arrived myself," the man said. "Not really even sure where we are."

There was no more time to talk. The Shadow Souled were everywhere. Jack ducked and swung Ashandar in an upward arc, slicing through a winged monster. From somewhere behind, he could hear Andreal's booming laughter.

It wasn't just the Shadow Souled that made the battle so unnerving. The land was turning against them. Jack had to step quickly so as not to sink into the softening ground. All around him, Awakened were falling.

Could we have come here only to die? His hands felt as if they were on fire as Ashandar sang to him. Jack danced among the dark servants; yet no matter how many fell, there were ten more.

He sliced through a vine as it wrapped around his leg, then backed away, holding Ashandar high, but a mighty tree swept toward him. Spindly vines shot out to pierce the ground, propelling it forward.

"Get down!" someone screamed.

Jack dropped low as an older boy leaped over him. "Parker?" Jack breathed.

Parker looked back and grinned. "It's good to see you, little brother!"

"Look out!" Jack cried as the spindly tree slammed into Parker, trampling him into the dirt.

"No!" Jack shrieked. He drew Ashandar and ran toward the tree. But before he'd gone three steps, something knocked him to the ground as a group of twenty or so men, women, and children tumbled to a stop all around him. *What's happening?* He ignored the newly arrived Awakened and spun around looking for the tree that had trampled Parker, but it was gone. His eyes scanned the madness, searching for any sign of his brother.

Another group of fifty or so Awakened materialized out of thin air, tumbling and then rising in a daze. It was happening throughout the valley.

"I've heard lots of stories about the mighty warrior Jack Staples, but so far all I've seen is you getting knocked off your feet."

"Parker!" Jack screamed.

His older brother stood before him tearing vines and dead branches from his body.

"It's good to see you … but let's talk when we're safely out of this mess." Parker nodded at something, and Jack turned to see a Shadule slithering toward them. The creature rose and unsheathed its bone-white blade in one fluid motion.

Jack lifted Ashandar and moved in, meeting the Shadule's lightning-quick strikes in movements that were as natural as breathing. From the corner of his eyes, he saw a large number of Clear Eyes appear out of nothing, but there was no time to understand it.

Though Alexia had traveled through a World Portal once before, she'd been unconscious and had no memory of it. Luckily, the Gang of Rogues told her what to expect, so Alexia inhaled the emerald sea, letting the liquid fill her lungs. Every breath brought life.

She looked down and saw her mother staring at her with wide eyes, as if she didn't understand what she was seeing. Alexia pulled her mother close, and for a long moment both women held each other in a fierce hug. Her mother leaned back and cupped Alexia's chin. Her hands were frigid, and her skin had a silvery quality to it, but she smiled warmly. Alexia couldn't remember the last time she'd been this happy. She wanted to tell her everything, but there was no talking in the emerald sea.

She watched Benaiah and Josiah treading water just beneath a river path. Both boys grinned and waved, then touched the river. Faster than Alexia could have imagined, they were whisked away in a streak of light.

Alexia clutched her mother's hand as the two women swam toward the river with Juno following close behind. The moment Alexia touched the stream, she was moving so fast, she thought her skin might burn off. It was exhilarating.

The ride was filled with twists and turns and sudden drops. Alexia screamed in delight, but only a trail of bubbles escaped her lips. Ahead was what looked like a tangle of thousands of bodies thrashing about in the darkness. Before she could make sense of it, Alexia was tumbling head over foot across muddied ground.

When she stopped, she pushed herself to her feet and nearly lost her head. A birdlike creature with swords for arms swung one of its blades wildly. A fierce-looking boy with orange-tinged eyes stepped in and kicked it in the chest.

"Wild!" Alexia gasped, but there was no time to say more. Five snout-nosed Oriax rushed at them with teeth bared, even as two winged Shadule attacked from above. Alexia drew her slim sword and went to work. The enemy was too close to make use of her sling. When a body pressed against her back, she was surprised to see her mother. Madeleine Dreager had an angry look in her eyes and had already found an ax.

Her mother kissed her on the forehead. "It's a dream come true to see you, my girl. We will catch up soon, but for now we fight!" Her mother moved with catlike grace as she leaped into the enemy and began working her ax. The enemy was upon them.

The Valley of Elah lay at the foot of a mountain nestled between two bluffs. Arthur's breath caught as the army of Awakened approached. Camped atop both bluffs were so many Shadow Souled, they outnumbered the sands of the sea.

A small battle raged in the center of the valley. A few thousand Awakened fought at least thirty thousand dark servants. The enemy atop the cliffs watched but didn't join. The Awakened would be finished soon enough without their help.

"It's a massacre," Sage whispered.

"We need to go now and rescue them," Arthur said.

"And if the army atop the bluffs decides to join the fight?" Eric asked.

"Then we fight them. We can't just sit here and watch our friends die."

"When a mother eagle shoves her baby from the nest," a voice said from behind Arthur, "it is precisely because she is sure of what she has not seen. Sometimes it is the faith of others that allows us to fly."

Arthur spun on his heel. "Mrs. Dumphry!" he shouted.

"Though I was sure you would rise to the challenge, it does not make me any less proud that you did." Mrs. Dumphry placed a hand on Arthur's shoulder. "If our friends in the valley are going to survive, I suggest you do not dally. A dallier today, a sluggard tomorrow."

Jack fought alongside Parker in a world of madness. Even with the miraculous arrival of the thousands of Awakened and Clear Eyes, they were hopelessly outnumbered. He gritted his teeth and lost himself in the movements—*spin, duck, twist, thrust, step back, deflect, thrust.*

He fought nine of the enemy at once as he tried to use his newest Soulprint to send them through time, but nothing happened. Three more dark servants joined the fight, and Jack could no longer stave them off. He stumbled on a root that hadn't been there a moment earlier and hit the ground hard.

Jack threw up his hands to shield himself as the ring of Time exploded in his chest. Suddenly he knew what to do. He didn't embrace his note but wrapped the melody around his enemy. A burst of light exploded around him, and the dark servants flew backward high into the air.

Parker stood over him, offering a hand. "What was that?"

"I figured it out is what it was." Jack grinned as Parker pulled him to his feet. "I sent them through time, to another place. I imagined an underground cavern somewhere deep in the earth." Before he could say another word, more dark servants were on them. Jack's movements changed as he stalked among his attackers. He wielded Ashandar with one arm, and every time he pointed his free arm at an attacker, it disappeared in a burst of light.

Before long the Shadow Souled were fleeing the boy with the black blade. A circle of clear space formed around Jack, but he didn't rest. He strode through the battlefield, searching for any Awakened needing his help. And then he saw her.

Alexia Dreager wielded her sword with a dizzying fury. Her friends from Belfast fought by her side, and hundreds of Clear Eyes kept the Shadow Souled from her back. Jack ran toward her but skidded to a stop when a creature appeared in front of him. He lifted his hand to send it away, but nothing happened. The creature had snakes' eyes and scaled skin, but otherwise looked like a young girl.

"Your Soulprint will not work on me." The creature's forked tongue flitted in and out as it spoke. Then it attacked. Jack had once thought the Shadule were impossibly quick, but they were nothing compared to this creature. Its every movement was a blur as Jack struggled to follow it from one moment to the next. He struck out with Ashandar, but the creature was already behind him. The creature sank its tiny fangs into Jack's flesh, every bite stinging like a scorpion.

Jack swung and swatted, kicked and punched, but he was always three moves behind. The bites were adding up. He listened for his note to take him away from the battlefield but heard nothing.

Covered in bites, Jack went to his knees. Ashandar dropped as he fell face forward in the dirt, unable to move. He felt a shiver of electricity pass over his body as a mammoth tree soared over Jack to crash into the creature. The creature hissed angrily and slithered away.

"Jack!" someone screamed. "I'm here." Arthur Greaves knelt beside him, but Jack couldn't move a muscle. Arthur heaved Jack over his back and began to run. "You're going to be all right. I promise. I just need to get you to Mrs. Dumphry!"

Alexia slammed the butt of her sword into the belly of a five-legged beast as Wild smashed his staff between the eyes of a goat-faced Oriax. The beasts crumbled, and both children spun with weapons ready. But the Shadow Souled were retreating. An army of Awakened had charged into the valley.

Alexia wiped her forehead and turned to Wild. "I'm so glad you're alive," she whispered.

"It's good to see you, too," he said.

"Alexia, would you like to introduce me to this young man?" Her mother stood a few paces away and watched with eyebrows raised.

Alexia squealed and leaped back. "Mother, this is Wild." She felt a burning in her cheeks. "He's a good friend. Wild, this is my mother."

Madeleine Dreager smiled. "I am very glad to meet you." She turned to Alexia. "I can't believe you're standing before me. It's all I've dreamed of."

Though the words were right, they sounded stiff to Alexia. *Mother is exhausted*, she thought. *She needs to rest!* She melted into her mother's arms. "Mother, why are you so cold?"

Her mother stepped back, a wary look in her eyes. "It is just the Assassin's poison leaving my body. I will be well soon."

"We need to go," Alexia said. Her eyes were on the rallying Shadow Souled. Thousands more had begun streaming into the valley.

"Arthur took Jack to see Mrs. Dumphry," Wild said. "I think he's hurt pretty bad."

"Arthur and Jack are here?" Alexia said. "And Mrs. Dumphry?"

"Yes. Mrs. Dumphry doesn't think the Shadow Army will attack once we're out of the valley. She thinks they're waiting for something. But we need to go before we become trapped again."

Chapter 21

A POT OF TEA

Arthur knelt by Jack's side. "Mrs. Dumphry is going to heal you, Jack. You're going to be okay."

Jack couldn't speak. He couldn't move a muscle, not even to blink. It was the strangest thing. Aside from being paralyzed, he felt perfectly healthy. His mind was clear, and he wasn't overly worried. More than anything, he was excited. Arthur, Parker, and Mrs. Dumphry were alive and well!

"He has been bitten by a Visperal," he heard Mrs. Dumphry say. "They are not deadly and are mostly used to keep prisoners from using their Soulprints. But in large doses, a Visperal's poison will cause paralysis for a time. Young Jack will be right as rain in a few minutes."

"Do you hear that, Jack?" Arthur shouted. "You'll be just fine. It will only take a few minutes!"

"I did not say he was deaf." Mrs. Dumphry sighed. "He is paralyzed. There is no need to shout."

Arthur nodded. "Right. You'll be just fine," he whispered. He grabbed Jack's head and turned it. "Did you see who else is here?"

Jack wanted to leap for joy. Alexia stood on the opposite side of the tent alongside an older woman with auburn hair. Mr. and Mrs. Greaves stood to the side, watching their son with a look of immense pride.

"Can you believe I found my parents? They've been searching for us almost since we left Ballylesson with Mrs. Dumphry. Their scales fell off the same day as mine; can you believe that? It's really quite amazing when you think about it. And you wouldn't believe what they've been doing even if I told you. It's a really long story, but I—"

"Madeleine Dreager," Mrs. Dumphry said, "I am very happy to see you alive." She met Alexia's eyes. "You did well, child. Very well indeed." She turned to Arthur's parents. "Augustus and Flannery, it makes my heart sing to see you again." Mrs. Dumphry turned her gaze back to Arthur. "But now is not the time for long stories."

"Right," Arthur said as he sat back down beside Jack. "Good point."

"Mrs. Dumphry," Alexia said, "how did you know my mother was alive? And how did you know I'd find Parker and Mr. Staples?"

"In truth, I wasn't certain of either. I have a Soulprint I am still discovering. I often get pictures in my mind or feelings in my heart about certain matters. In some small way, my Soulprint gives me windows into the future. As for your mother, I saw a picture of her.

She was wrapped in chains and locked in a steel box hidden beneath the Assassin's throne."

"We found her strapped to the ceiling," Alexia said.

"The Assassin often moved me," Madeleine said hurriedly.

Mrs. Dumphry offered a tight smile. "I'm just glad Alexia was able to find you."

"What happened to you?" Wild asked. "When we were thrown through time, when and where did you go?"

"Ah, now that is a fun story." Mrs. Dumphry chuckled. "I went back to the beginning."

Though he still couldn't move, Jack could once again feel his body, and he was relatively certain drool was dripping from his chin.

"To the beginning of what?" Arthur asked.

"To my beginning," she said. "I arrived five thousand, twenty-four years ago, just a minute or so before my birth."

"Why would anyone want to see that?" Arthur made a face.

"Not to the day of my first birth"—Mrs. Dumphry sighed—"but to the day my scales fell off. I arrived in the throne room and saw myself stab the poet. And I saw him forgive me." She smiled in delight. "I can only surmise I was taken there because I was thinking of the moment as we began to travel."

"Wait, how many years?" Arthur asked.

"You mean that you lived all those years again?" Alexia said.

"I did." Mrs. Dumphry's smile broadened. "And I must say, I had far more fun the second time. I'd always wondered about the moment after the poet saved Aias and me from the Assassin. So this time, I hid behind one of the pillars and watched him. When the Assassin left, I followed him out of the throne room."

Jack remembered the moment. He'd been there with Time and had seen it too. When the Assassin left the throne room, a small figure in a hooded cloak had scurried out after him. *Was that Mrs. Dumphry?*

"It wasn't just the Poet's Coffer the Assassin stole that day," Mrs. Dumphry continued. "He took something else."

It took all of his energy, but Jack managed a slow, deliberate blink.

"I have always been intrigued by the blood of the poet. Before Jack's sword fell into a pool of the poet's blood, it was a blade no different than any other. But when it touched the blood, it became Ashandar. The poet's cloak was also covered in his blood. Alexia's cloak and the Atherial Cloaks that Elion gave you all came from material taken from the poet's patchwork cloak."

Jack tried to lick his lips but only managed to shove more drool from his mouth.

"The Assassin knew the poet's blood was dangerous, though I doubt he understood how dangerous. After the poet whisked us away, the Assassin gathered the blood into a vial and hid it in a cavern near the very foundations of our world. It took me almost three thousand years to find it."

"You spent three thousand years traveling through underground caverns?" Arthur rocked on his heels.

"I did," she said cheerily. "Yet I thought it might take five thousand years or more, so you can imagine my delight when I found it and had more than two thousand years to spare."

Arthur opened his mouth, then closed it again.

"What have you been doing since?" Alexia leaned forward.

"A little of this, a little of that," Mrs. Dumphry said. "I took up sewing. I traveled through Africa and learned a number of fabulous new dances."

Jack waited for more, but nothing came. *Sewing and dancing?* He could blink easily now and wag his tongue, but his limbs still wouldn't move, and he couldn't make a sound.

"It hasn't all been a holiday. I managed to raise an army. They should be here within the hour."

"How many are coming?" Wild asked.

"Almost half a million, all told."

"That be the biggest army the world has ever been seeing!" Andreal clapped his hands together.

"I have even more good news," Mrs. Dumphry said. "I also passed a very large and impressive jungle that was making its way toward the valley. I'm not certain, but I think it originated in Brazil of all places! Besides the army and the jungle, I saw a vast number of Clear Eyes traveling here. I don't know how many are coming, but I'd guess they will outnumber the humans."

Everyone sat with mouths agape.

"A jungle is coming?" Arthur's voice squeaked.

"It will be a battle like the world has never known," Honi whispered.

"Yes," Mrs. Dumphry said. "It truly is a sad day for our world."

A groan escaped Jack's lips as his fingers twitched.

"Jack!" Arthur shouted. "He's trying to say something!"

Jack screamed as a jolt of adrenaline surged through him, and he stood up panting as if he'd just run the hundred-meter dash. "Wow," he said breathlessly.

Arthur hugged him. "It's so good to see you, Jack." Then all the joy melted from his face. "I didn't want to tell you while you were like that. But we need to find Parker. You both need to hear what I have to say."

"What happened?" Jack said, feeling numb. "Where's my father?" In truth, he already knew. He could see it in Arthur's eyes.

Alexia wasn't sure, but she thought Mr. Staples might be dead. *If so, it'll be the second time I've lost my father.* Her heart sank at the thought even as it broke for Jack.

She and her mother leaned against a thick tree. Madeleine Dreager stared into her daughter's eyes. "I've missed you, Alexia. I could barely believe my eyes when that monster brought you into the throne room. I …"—her mother wiped away tears—"I hadn't thought life could become any more miserable."

"You saw me?" Alexia tried to shove down the shame rising inside her. She hadn't wanted her mother to know she'd been deceived by the Assassin.

"I watched everything. The Assassin promised he'd make you curse my memory. I don't understand why you chose to follow him. I thought we'd raised you better than that!"

Alexia brushed her tears with the back of her hand. "I'm sorry, Mother. I was so confused. I thought Korah was Father. I never wanted to disappoint you!"

"I was disappointed." A cold look entered Madeleine Dreager's eyes. Then after a moment, she smiled. "But it's all right. You rescued me, and that is worth something." Her mother cupped her cheek.

"Mother, your hand is so cold!" Alexia gasped. "Are you all right?"

Her mother whipped her hand away. "I'm perfectly fine. I've already told you; it's just the Assassin's poison leaving my body." In the light of the torch, Alexia's mother almost sparkled.

"If you need something, I'm sure Mrs. Dumphry could—"

"I said I'm fine," she snapped. "No need to bother the old woman. I will be well in a few hours."

Alexia stared at her mother for a long moment. She truly was a beautiful and strong woman. Yet there was an edge to her that hadn't been there before. *Being tortured by the Assassin for years will do that to a person.*

"What happened that day?" Alexia said. "How did you escape from Korah, and how did they find you again? I saw some of it through Korah's Memory Stone, but I still don't understand."

A faraway look entered her mother's eyes. "My Soulprint allows me to switch places with someone, so long as they are willing. Except when I reappear, I arrive not where they are but where they were a few minutes earlier. Your father switched places with me, and I appeared in the kitchen of our house. I ran into the woods in hopes of finding you, and instead I found Miel. I trusted her. I begged her to help me save your father. When I turned my back, she attacked. Korah and Miel took me to Thaltorose on the very same day."

Jack and Parker sat together inside the large tent. "I can't believe he's gone," Parker said. "I didn't think anything could kill him."

The familiar hollow feeling of losing a parent settled inside Jack.

"I'm going to make him pay," Jack said. "I'm going to end the Assassin once and for all."

"I know you're not a child anymore," Parker said, "and I have no doubt you're as strong as Mother and Father always said you'd be. But do you really think you can kill the Assassin?"

"I don't know. But the prophecy says Alexia and I will defeat him"—Jack grimaced—"right around the time we destroy the world."

"I don't know that there's going to be much left to destroy." The earth trembled as if in response to Parker's words.

"I'm sorry, boys, but I must interrupt." Mrs. Dumphry stood in the tent entrance. "Time has grown too short, and we must fight even as we grieve." She stepped inside, and the rest of the group followed.

"The Great Awakening has come, and every scale has fallen from the eyes of human and beast. In every country and town, the Awakened fight the Shadow Souled, and the Awakened are losing." Mrs. Dumphry placed a pot of water on the fire as everyone sat. "The Assassin's Shadow has stolen hope and replaced it with fear. The few remaining forests, mountains, and valleys still loyal to the Author are being destroyed. The seven oceans boil as the sea creatures clash. Yet it is here in the Valley of Elah that the war will be decided.

The Assassin has chosen the battleground where he will meet the Children of Prophecy."

"Why here?" Arthur asked.

"I think he chose this valley because it is special to the Author. It was his home when he first came to our world."

"Why have the earthquakes slowed?" Jack asked. "Even the weather seems normal. Doesn't that mean we're winning?"

"I'm afraid not. It's the Awakened who gather in this place, the earth and air, the trees, flowers, and insects—all have journeyed here to fight beside us. But this is no Oasis. It is a last stand."

"So what are the Shadow Souled waiting for?" Wild asked. "If they attacked now, they could crush us. Their scouts must have told them more Awakened are coming."

"I do not know," Mrs. Dumphry said. "But they are waiting for something. I fear the Assassin has spun a web, and I have yet to decipher his plans."

"Oh!" Jack stood and rummaged through his satchel. He pulled out the small tin he'd taken from beneath Mrs. Dumphry's desk in Ballylesson and offered it to her. "I can't believe I forgot. It wasn't easy, but we retrieved this for you."

Mrs. Dumphry smiled as she took the tin. "Ah, how I have missed this! Thank you both. It means the world to me." She opened it and brought it close to her nose, inhaling deeply. "Now, who would like some tea?"

"Tea?" Jack said. "I don't understand. What does it do?"

"It quenches thirst, for one thing!" Mrs. Dumphry said. "A good tea will also help calm the nerves and relax the mind. And this is my very favorite tea in all the world."

"We risked our lives for tea? It won't hurt the Assassin or something?"

"Oh, I doubt it. He may not like the taste, but I wouldn't share it with him even if he did." Mrs. Dumphry laughed at her own joke. "The tea was only part of the reason I sent you to Ballylesson."

Jack waited as Mrs. Dumphry poured the leaves and spices into the pot of water that was already boiling on the fire. The smell of mint, jasmine, and something Jack couldn't quite place filled the air.

"Well what was the other reason?" Jack asked.

"You needed a chance to lead. You needed to be shoved from the nest so you could test those wings of yours. A leader who has never led is merely an 'er.' Seeing as you are alive and have arrived safely, my plan obviously worked. Besides, I very much wanted to drink this tea at least once more before the end of the world." She stirred the pot with a wooden spoon. "I have no doubt your time in Ballylesson taught you some very important things. Now, I won't offer again. Would anyone like a cup?"

Chapter 22

THE BEGINNING
OF THE END

A fearful look entered Madeleine Dreager's eyes, and she let out a low hiss as she turned toward the tent entrance. "Mother, what's wrong?" Alexia whispered.

"I need to leave." Her mother stood up quickly, causing the conversation to stop. "I'm sorry," she said, "but I'm not feeling well. I need some fresh air." Her nose twitched as if she could smell something the others could not.

"Of course," Mrs. Dumphry said. Alexia wanted to follow her mother, but Mrs. Dumphry's attention turned to her. "Child, what do you know of the Clear Eyes?"

"What do you mean?" Alexia asked, watching her mother go.

"I told you about the vast number of Clear Eyes making their way here. Never before have the animals mobilized into an army. Though they fight the Shadow Souled, until today we thought most Clear Eyes were too wild to fight together. Yet while you fought in the valley, it was clear they were fighting to protect you."

"Oh, that," Alexia said. "They have a prophecy about me as well. They call me Star Child, and their prophecy says they will fight by my side in the Final Hunt, which is what they call the Last Battle."

Every eye widened as it fixed on Alexia. "You can talk to them? To all of them?" Mrs. Dumphry leaned in.

Alexia hesitated. "It's one of my new Soulprints, though I'm still learning how to use it."

"Remarkable," Mrs. Dumphry said. "Elion can talk to the animals, but never before has a human had such an ability. Child, tell us what you know of—"

Gasps escaped every mouth as Elion stepped into the tent. The Sephari smiled when her eyes landed on Jack and Alexia. "It is good to see you both, to see all of you." She nodded to the group. "I wanted to come days ago, but travel has become almost impossible."

"It is very good to see you." Mrs. Dumphry hugged Elion. "I had been worried we would have to face the Assassin without you."

"Who did ye bring with ye?" Andreal rumbled as Mrs. Dumphry sat back down.

"I have gathered every last giant and Sephari on this earth. In all, there are one hundred and seven of my race who have come, and more than twelve thousand giants."

"I would no have believed it could be done!" Andreal smacked a fist into his hand. "Giants have no fought beside humans fer thousands of years. Ye truly do be a miracle worker!"

Elion nodded. "And from what I have been told, thanks to Arthur Greaves we also have the Poet's Coffer."

"And we have this." Mrs. Dumphry pulled out the vial of the poet's blood.

Elion's eyes shifted to a rich green color. "I would love to hear the story of how you found it, but that will have to wait for another time. It seems we are ready to face the Assassin. Now we must strategize a way to draw him out."

"His hordes hold the high ground," Mrs. Dumphry said. "But we mustn't go to them. If we fight them in the valley, we'll be crushed between the two armies. We must find a way to make them come to us."

Alexia's mother appeared in the tent entrance just behind Elion.

"Even with our armies, we are vastly outnumbered," Elion said. "But if we fight with wisdom, the battle is not lost. The world is—"

Madeleine Dreager brandished a pale, jagged blade, and Elion's eyes blazed royal blue as her hair rose from her shoulders. The Sephari spun, but by the time she'd turned, the blade was already deep in her chest.

For a moment no one moved. Elion sank to her knees as Madeleine Dreager pulled out the blade, then pounced into the midst of the Awakened, swinging it in a flurry of strikes and stabs.

Alexia backed away from the scene. "No!" she cried. "Mother, what are you doing?"

Her mother vaulted into the corner of the tent as Honi, Parker, and Andreal approached with weapons bared. Jack unsheathed Ashandar as electrified sparks snapped and popped across Arthur's skin.

"Your Sephari witch is dead!" Madeleine snarled.

Mrs. Dumphry was on her knees, staring at the festering wound in her side. "What you have done"—her voice came out in a whisper—"should not have been possible." Her eyes drifted to Elion, who lay flat on her back staring blankly at the tent ceiling. All light had faded from her eyes.

"Mother, no!" Alexia wept.

"The Shadow Lord wanted to get your attention." A silvery sheen rippled across Madeleine's skin as she showed Mrs. Dumphry the pale blade. "This weapon is the only thing my master brought with him from Siyyon. It was forged from the stone of the Sacred Mountain." She contorted, twisting inward. It wasn't Madeleine Dreager standing before them but a Grendall, with silvery skin and large oval mirrors for eyes. It turned to Alexia. "Did you truly think you could rescue your mother so easily? That the Dark Lord didn't know you were there?"

Alexia struggled to breathe. The Assassin had used her to sneak the Grendall into the Council. The creature's eyes misted and became a window to another place. Alexia saw her mother and James Staples wrapped in shadows and floating at the top of a mountain.

"Father?" Jack cried.

"If you ever want to see your parents alive," the Grendall said, "then both Children of Prophecy must meet the Lord of Shadows at the top of the mountain. The Lord of Death demands you come alone and you come immediately. Join my master and watch him remake the world in his image! Come and see—"

The creature staggered back, falling into the tent as an arrow struck it. Alexia turned to see Wild with bow in hand. "I'd heard about enough of that," he said.

Alexia stumbled to Mrs. Dumphry and knelt by her side. "I'm sorry," Alexia cried. "I didn't know!"

"I, too, was deceived, child. Remember, it was I who sent you to get her." Mrs. Dumphry's voice was weak as the wound in her side turned black. "There is no shame in not knowing, only in not doing once we know. Now"—her lips quivered as the blackness spread—"the both of you were born for this moment." Her gaze shifted between Alexia and Jack. "I was born to prepare you for it. If I am dying, it means I have been successful. And that means I can die happy." She reached into her cloak and handed Alexia the small vial of the poet's blood. "You must use this at the opportune time." She gasped as the blackness spread up her neck. "Do not grieve for me. I have lived a thousand lifetimes, and I am ready. Every moment spent in regret is like a frog that believes itself a t—" The blackness spread across her face as Mrs. Dumphry exhaled her last breath.

For a long moment, nobody moved. All eyes shifted between the two bodies. Andreal dropped to his knees as Honi crumbled beside Elion. Neither man nor giant tried to hide his tears.

"Gone," Andreal whispered. "I did no think it possible." His gaze shifted to Elion. "But to be losing both …"

"The Last Battle will be the end of the world," Honi said. "How can we defeat him when we have suffered such losses before ever entering the battlefield?"

Rage pooled in Alexia as she stared at the two bodies. *How many times can the Assassin steal my parents from me?* She began to shake.

"No"—Jack pushed tears from his eyes—"I don't believe it. I won't believe it! Mrs. Dumphry and Elion didn't fight all those years so we could give up now." He studied the vial in Alexia's hands. "We have the coffer, and we have the pen to open it. And now we have the poet's blood. I don't know what any of it means, but we can't give up." He clenched his fists. "Besides, I won't leave my father to that monster."

"You can't be thinking of meeting the Assassin on the mountain-top?" Wild stood. "You know it's a trap."

Alexia stood in a cold rage. "I don't care," she said. "We're going to spring his trap and finish this once and for all."

"Then I'm going with you," Wild said.

"No," Jack said. "The Assassin said he'd kill our parents if we didn't come alone. Alexia and I are meant to do this. It was proph-esied before the world began."

"I'm coming, Jack. I don't care—"

"No," Alexia said. "Jack's right. We have to do it alone." Alexia couldn't bear the thought of watching Wild die. She had no doubt she and Jack would be running to their deaths. But she wouldn't watch Wild die first.

Wild nodded. "All right. The prophecy says the Children of Prophecy will lead the Awakened in the Last Battle. I will follow your lead."

"I am sorry." Honi stood. "I should not have said what I did. And you are right. No matter the odds, we must continue to fight."

"We'll need be getting ye to the base of the mountain, then." Andreal stood and fingered his axes.

"It will be a slaughter," Arthur said. "If we enter the valley, we'll be crushed between the two armies."

"I'm sure that's what the Assassin wants. But the only battle that matters is the one with the Assassin himself," Wild said. "If we can get Alexia and Jack to the mountain, that will be enough. It has to be."

"Gather everyone." Alexia turned to Jack. "You lead the Awakened. I'll lead the Clear Eyes." Her eyes drifted to the Grendall's lifeless body. "We leave now."

An army of more than a million Awakened stood behind Jack. It consisted of men, women, and children of every age. The youngest he'd seen was a four-year-old girl with white hair and piercing blue eyes; the oldest, a man who must have been in his nineties. When the world itself was at stake, every last person was needed.

On Jack's right, his sister rode atop an enormous grizzly. Woven into her hair was a garland of fresh flowers, and gathered behind were a vast number of Clear Eyes that easily outnumbered the humans. Winged animals soared above.

To Jack's left was everything else—a hundred and seven Sephari, twelve thousand giants, and a jungle. When he'd arrived in the valley, there'd been no trees in sight, but now there were tens of thousands of towering trees with thick canopies. Bushes, plants, and flowers grew between, and swarms of insects and crawling plants were scattered throughout. It looked as if they'd grown there for centuries.

"What do you mean she's your sister?" Arthur said.

"I mean we have the same parents," Jack said.

"What else would it mean?" Parker added.

Arthur worked his mouth as he looked from Jack to Parker. "You're joking, right?"

Jack and his brother laughed as Arthur threw his hands in the air. "I can't go into the Last Battle not knowing if you're joking or not."

"I'll tell you once we get to the mountain," Jack said. He turned his attention to Alexia and nodded. She offered a tight smile and nodded back. In the sky above, Jack's and Alexia's stars brightened visibly, piercing the slithering darkness. Jack raised Ashandar as a thunderous shout rose from behind. Alexia stood atop her bear, and every Clear Eye roared, whinnied, snorted, and gruffed.

Jack broke into a run. He didn't need to look back to know that the army followed close on his heels. The air around him was pure and the ground solid. From the corner of his eye, he saw the Clear Eyes. Alexia and her Gang of Rogues were the only humans who rode atop the animals, and they quickly outpaced the humans.

Hundreds of giants bounded past Jack, yet Andreal remained by his side. All his friends matched his stride. He knew their goal wasn't to destroy the enemy; it was to make sure Jack got to the base of the mountain. Every one of them was willing to die if it meant Jack might live. *But I won't let them!* It was a grim thought. *Enough people have died for me already.*

If he hadn't been so filled with adrenaline, Jack would have stopped to look. The hundred and seven Sephari flew above, chanting the most haunting and horrifying cadence he'd ever heard. Their song was death, and Jack felt pity for any dark servant who faced them. The Sephari hadn't taken Elion's murder well. Off to Jack's left, the entire jungle was moving, the rolling roots of the trees propelling them forward.

Jack eyed the cliff tops. The Shadow Souled waited on the edges, but so far they hadn't moved. Not until the army of Awakened neared the center of the valley did a bleary horn sound. Both bluffs turned black as millions of the Assassin's servants rushed down. *This was the Assassin's plan. He demands we come to him but ensures the destruction of the Awakened in the process of getting us there.* Swarms of plagued insects, rot-ridden forests, and creeping plants descended the ridge. Shadule, Oriax, Drogule, and distorted beasts too numerous to count charged in. Snarling, pale-faced humans of every age joined the biggest army the world had ever seen. Tornadoes formed among the ranks of darkness, and even as they swept in, many of the Shadow Souled were flung aside. A great fissure opened in the side of the cliff.

The first ranks of the dark army crashed over the Awakened. Mrs. Dumphry had been right: to meet the enemy in the valley was a ridiculous battle strategy. There was no chance of retreat.

Jack strode through the melee, not allowing himself to see what was happening. The only hope for the Awakened was if the Children of Prophecy made it to the top of the mountain. He couldn't stay behind and help. Unless he and Alexia were able to defeat the Assassin, the war was lost.

Alexia forced more than a million images from her mind. Far quicker than she'd have thought possible, her ability to communicate with the Clear Eyes had become second nature. She could see through the eyes of any animal, or all of them if she wished, and she could understand their thoughts. Some communicated through images, some through vibrations or smells or a mixture of all of it. Alexia had no problem deciphering it.

A winged Shadule swept over, yet Alexia felt no fear. She'd never been this angry or heartbroken in her life. Elion and Mrs. Dumphry had been killed because she'd been stupid enough to bring the enemy into their camp. Guilt tore through her as she leaped from the grizzly's back.

Alexia soared, clinging to the shrieking Shadule. It wrapped its clawed fingers around her neck, but she struck it with the pale blade, the same blade the Grendall had used on Elion and Mrs. Dumphry. She'd taken it, intending to use it on the Assassin. Alexia dropped back down atop the grizzly as the Shadule tumbled lifelessly to the ground behind her.

The grizzly galloped toward the base of the mountain. Alexia whispered into the bear's ear, urging him on. A spear-bearing Shadule swept down, but before it could attack, a winged lion crashed into it. Alexia sent a stone into an ostrich-faced Oriax as a camel trotted past and kicked away a pig-snouted wolverine. Vines shot from the earth to wrap around the grizzly, but the bear was too strong. It ran through them.

"Watch out!" Josiah called.

Alexia turned as a thorny branch slammed into her chest. She fell from the grizzly as her Gang of Rogues surrounded her. Juno threw out an arm and hoisted Alexia up to sit behind her on a giraffe. The giraffe leaped forward, and Alexia's gang spread out on either side, forming a protective circle around her.

Arthur sent fifty bolts of lightning exploding into the ranks of Shadow Souled as he ran beside Jack. Whenever a dark servant came too close, Jack battled it with Ashandar or sent it away in a burst of light and wind. Wild worked his quarterstaff, Andreal wielded both half-mooned axes like a madman, and Honi thrust his walking staff in wide circles, striking the Shadow Souled and sending golden sparks along the dark servants' skin as they fell.

In the midst of the insanity, Arthur was most amazed with his parents. His father expertly wielded a sword with a blade that was twice as long as Arthur. Even the Shadule were thrust aside by the brute force of the thing. Though Arthur couldn't understand what his mother was doing, she took down twice as many dark servants as his father, working her knitting needles as she marched through the madness. By the looks of it, she was knitting Arthur a new coat. Each time an enemy came close, she flicked a needle toward it, and the enemy was hurled away as if had been hit by a mammoth fist.

The ground split open, threatening to swallow Arthur and his friends, but before they dropped more than a pace, the earth fought back. A bridge of ice formed beneath them. Arthur shared an amazed look with Jack as they ran along the ice.

This battle was far different from the one in the Quagmire. While most of the world fought to destroy them, some of the earth was fighting to save them. The ice bridge shattered as lava shot upward, but this time Arthur was ready with a platform of light. Fifty trees blocked their way, and Parker screamed as he leaped into them. The trees trampled Jack's older brother, then suddenly dried up and burst apart, leaving him miraculously unharmed.

The Sephari were everywhere, wielding slim blades in a fury that pushed back dark servants and trees with equal ease. They ran through the air, each footprint leaving colored mist as their song resounded through the valley.

"We're nearing the base of the mountain," Parker called back. "Only a short distance farther, and—" An Oriax slammed into Parker, hurling him away.

"Parker!" Arthur screamed.

"No!" Jack shouted. He fought his way toward where Parker had fallen. Arthur's shield of light formed around Jack as he knelt over his brother.

Blood seeped from Parker's mouth as his lifeless eyes stared blankly at the slithering sky. "No!" Jack screamed at the mountain. "I won't let you have him!" He closed his eyes and embraced his note, soaring through time.

When Jack's feet hit the ground, he arrived a few seconds earlier and stood behind his brother in the midst of the Shadow Souled. He spun and sent a hundred of them hurling through space and time. "How dare you try and take my brother from me," he screamed.

"We're nearing the base of the mountain," Parker called to the Jack from a few seconds earlier. "Only a short distance farther, and we'll be there!" And in one smooth motion, Jack dispatched the Oriax.

Parker stared at the lifeless Oriax a moment and then at Jack. "What did you just do?"

"I won't let the Assassin have you, too." Jack hugged his brother. Suddenly he felt as if someone had kicked him in the gut. In the space of a single breath, the oxygen was gone.

Alexia gasped as all oxygen left the air. Juno clutched her throat as every Awakened and Clear Eyes, every Shadow Souled stumbled to a stop, choking on nothing. The giraffe collapsed, and Alexia landed next to a wheezing Shadule. She rose to her knees, but the corners of her vision were darkening.

A short distance away, a crack ripped through the earth. Tears streamed from her eyes as thousands of Clear Eyes, Awakened, and dark servants were swallowed up. Alexia fell facedown in the dirt, gagging. A cool wind whipped through, and with it came fresh oxygen. The valley began to move as animal, human, and creature filled their lungs.

Alexia pulled Juno to her feet and hurled the pale blade into a rising Shadule. She strode over and yanked the blade free as her gang gathered round. "We're almost there!" Alexia shouted as the Clear Eyes galloped, leaped, slithered, and soared around them in a circle of protection.

The Valley of Elah boiled as the Awakened, Clear Eyes, and jungle fought to move to the mountain. Arthur formed his light into a battering ram and slammed it into the chest of a Drogule. The monster dropped to its knees as Arthur and his friends darted past. Arthur struck a turtle-faced Oriax with a streak of lightning as Jack sent fifty Shadow Souled away in a burst of wind and light. The Sephari anthem resounded above the roar of battle, but the song diminished each time one of them died. Everywhere Arthur looked, the Awakened were being defeated. Flaming trees thrashed about in a high-pitched keening. The Shadow Souled climbed atop the giants, taking them down scores at a time. Creeping vines strangled the crawling plants, and swarms of Awakened butterflies, ladybugs, crickets, and more were swallowed in thick clouds of plague-ridden insects.

Arthur and Jack stumbled as they reached the black rock. "We made it!" Jack gasped. Arthur turned to see his parents, Sage, Aliyah, and the others arrive with another thousand or so Awakened, trees, giants, and Sephari. The Awakened formed ranks four deep to keep the enemy back—and suddenly Arthur and Jack had no one to fight. They stood on their toes, searching for Alexia.

"She should be here by now," Arthur shouted.

"There!" Jack pointed. Fifty winged Shadule circled an area a short distance away. Thousands of Clear Eyes fought to keep them back but were hopelessly outnumbered. "Alexia must be in there somewhere." Jack's hand tightened on Ashandar.

"No." Wild placed a hand on Jack's shoulder. "Let us go get her. We can't risk you going back into the middle of this. You need to go up the mountain."

Jack shook his head. "I'm not going anywhere without my sister." With a dangerous look in his eyes, he turned and strode back into the madness.

"You must have drawn every Shadule in the Assassin's army!" Josiah shouted. At least fifty of the creatures circled above, and another hundred or more slithered around the menagerie of Clear Eyes.

"They smell the Poet's Coffer," Alexia called as she sliced a Shadule across the ribs. Arthur had insisted that one of the Children of Prophecy should carry the coffer into battle, and Jack had been adamant that Alexia be the one to carry it. As she fought now, she was sure the coffer was helping her in some way. She was far less exhausted than she should have been. The small wooden box radiated energy as it vibrated in her cloak pocket.

Benaiah was everywhere. He fought with two long blades, and the boy was unstoppable. He spun, kicked, and leaped about, landing on the back of a Shadule and striking it even as he leaped to the next. Alexia knew Summer could heal with her Soulprint, but as she fought by Alexia's side, she did the opposite. Summer had no weapon; she turned in a slow circle as she walked. Every Shadule that came close dropped as if utterly exhausted. Juno fought with unbelievable skill. Flames danced along her whip, and where it struck, the enemy dropped like stones. Addy's Soulprint wasn't one of war, and though the small girl wielded her knives with precision, she stayed close to Josiah, who spent much of his energy fighting to protect her.

Three Shadule struck at the same time. Alexia spun in a tight circle, the Assassin's blade taking care of two of the creatures even as Juno's whip dispatched the third. "I don't think we're going to make it!" Juno said through gritted teeth.

Tens of thousands of Clear Eyes were dying every second, and each death was a knife to Alexia's heart. She was the Star Child; she'd led them into the Final Hunt, and they were being slaughtered. Alexia glanced toward the mountain. *So close!* Twenty Shadule exploded away in a burst of light as wind whipped at her cloak.

"Jack!" she shouted. Her brother strode through the madness, striking out with Ashandar. A spindly vine shot from the earth to wrap around her neck, but another thick, green vine ripped it away.

Wild, Arthur, and many more Awakened followed just behind Jack. Alexia and her gang didn't waste a second; they sprinted toward the base of the mountain as the Clear Eyes protected their backs.

As they stepped onto the black rock of the mountain, Jack hugged Alexia for a moment, then stepped away. "We need to go," he said. "Every second we wait, more of the Awakened will die."

Alexia stepped back, and turned to her gang and nodded. "Thank you," she said. "For everything. You are the best friends I could have hoped for." She turned to Arthur, saying, "You are the most courageous person I've ever met." Without allowing herself to think, Alexia stepped forward and kissed Wild on the cheek. "Thank you for always looking out for me," she whispered. Wild's cheeks flushed.

Jack stepped back from Arthur and Parker, then turned to Alexia. "What do you say, Sister, should we go destroy the Assassin?"

"I'll race you to the top," she said. Jack nodded, and both children broke into a run.

Chapter 23

THE FULLNESS

Jack Staples and Alexia Dreager ascended the mountain, each step sending black shale tumbling down. After a few minutes of running, they slowed to a walk as reality sank in. "You know he'll never let them live," Jack said.

"I know," Alexia said. "He is going to kill them both, and then he's going to kill us."

Jack didn't respond. He knew they couldn't stop. This was what they'd been born to do, to face the Assassin in the Last Battle.

Earthquakes rattled the foundations of the world, yet the mountain remained relatively still. A great roar sounded, and Jack turned to see stars falling from the heavens. The first star to hit the earth careened into the distant ocean, sending a vast tsunami crashing toward shore. A nearby mountain erupted, spraying volcanic ash and lava. The world was breaking, and there was no stopping it.

Jack shared a fearful look with his sister before continuing upward. They topped a false summit, and there lurked the demon Belial. It waited in the shadow of the mountain, with James Staples and Madeleine Dreager on either side. One of the demon's thick feelers was wrapped around each of their necks.

Though the demon was in no way similar to the diamond-skinned Assassin he'd fought twice before, Jack was sure it was the same wretched being. No earthly creature could be so purely evil as what hulked before him now—a sickly thing of beaks, claws, tentacles, and one dripping eye. Both Madeleine Dreager and James Staples watched their children with fear-filled eyes, but they couldn't speak.

"Dare to look upon my handiwork!" the demon wheezed. "The end has come! A world reformed in my image." The world crumbled as lightning, hurricanes, fires, and tsunamis filled the horizon. The battle still raged in the valley, but it was clear the Awakened would soon be finished.

The demon laughed as the mountain shook.

From what Arthur could see, only a handful of giants were still alive. Even more chilling, the Sephari song had ended minutes ago, cutting off abruptly. The few thousand Awakened still standing fought with their backs to the mountain against the innumerable hordes of darkness. Arthur peered toward the top of the mountain. *If you're going to do something, you need to do it soon!* If they were lucky, the Awakened might last another hour.

A number of trees and crawling plants still fought, though most were on fire. They didn't stay together like the humans and animals but flowed through the Shadow Souled, thrashing about wildly.

"There's not going to be anything left to save!" Sage hollered as she leaped over Arthur and sunk her claws into a Shadule, hurling it away.

Arthur nodded as a nearby mountain exploded in an eruption of lava and ash. He formed a shield and stretched it out to cover as many of the Awakened as possible. He dropped to his knees as a heavy weight suddenly pressed down on every part of his body. Whatever was forcing him to the ground was also affecting everything. Tree branches began snapping as winged Clear Eyes and monsters rocketed to the ground.

"What's happening?" he cried.

"It's the gravity," Honi groaned. "It's fighting against us!"

Everything in the valley was being crushed. *The Assassin is killing his own followers!* Arthur couldn't tear his eyes away from the shelled bugs that had been biting at him a moment earlier. They imploded as their hard shells cracked and squished inward. *How do we fight gravity?* It was a frantic thought. Arthur groaned as he pushed himself upward. He felt as heavy as a house but managed to climb to his knees.

A great popping sound exploded across the valley, and suddenly Arthur was as light as air. He'd been pressing so hard against the ground, he was thrust upward and didn't come back down. Arthur screamed as he slammed into a canopy of branches. A thorny branch swatted him away, and he crashed into a rising Sage, bringing them both to the ground. Rock, earth, Awakened, and Shadow Souled ascended all around them.

"Grab my hand!" his father shouted. Arthur's father gripped a thick vine that kept him from floating up. Arthur reached for his father as the gravity righted itself and the world crashed back down.

This is the end, Arthur thought as he and Sage landed in a heap. *There is no fighting gravity.*

"Let them go!" Jack shouted. "If you hurt them, I'll—"

"You are not in command here, boy," the demon wheezed as it slumped to the edge of a great precipice. The demon lifted James Staples and Madeleine Dreager so they hovered over the sheer drop. "All you have ever been is the Author's puppet. He used you to fight me, and now you have failed." The demon's leaking eye turned to survey the world. "Can't you see? Before long the only thing left in this world will be the mountain beneath your feet. It is over! I have won the War of Time. If the Author ever cared about this world, he would have fought by your side. But where is he? Why hasn't he come to your rescue? The decision is yours, Children of Prophecy," the demon wheezed. "Bow before me, and I will command my armies to retreat. Bend your knees, and I will free your parents. You can still save what's left of your pathetic world."

Jack placed a hand on Ashandar, and the demon tightened its feelers. Jack's father and Alexia's mother gasped and began turning blue. "Drop your blade, boy."

"Jack," Alexia said, "I don't know if that's truly your father or my mother, but he can't be trusted."

"I know," Jack said sadly. "But what choice do we have?" He tossed Ashandar forward so it landed at the feet of the Assassin, clanging on the black stone.

The demon let out a gurgling laugh. "Kneel. Worship your new god, and I will spare them."

Jack met Alexia's eyes and nodded. She grabbed his hand, and together the Children of Prophecy stepped forward. Jack embraced the ring of Time, and he and his sister soared back a few seconds to appear just in front of the Assassin. Jack caught Ashandar before it clanged at the demon's feet. Beside him, Alexia's sling was already spinning as she hurled the vial of the poet's blood at the demon's chest.

Belial moved quicker than lightning and swatted the vial to the ground. Before Jack's blade could strike true, an unseen feeler swept his feet from under him while another feeler yanked Ashandar from his hands and hurled it away.

Jack and his sister tried to scramble away, but the demon's appendages wrapped around their legs and yanked upward so both children hung upside down next to their parents. Alexia hurled her pale blade at the demon, but Belial shifted away and the blade tumbled down the mountain.

"Pathetic," the demon rasped. "To think that the two of you were the last hope for humanity."

Jack and Alexia shared a look of horror. This had been their only plan.

James Staples and Madeleine Dreager kicked frantically as the demon lifted them high into the air. "No!" Jack and Alexia screamed in unison as their parents dropped into the darkness.

"No," Jack moaned.

"Now, witness the fullness of my power," the demon croaked. "See what it is I have truly been fighting for."

Hanging upside down across from his sister, Jack felt as if he could see forever. Everywhere he looked, the world crumbled. Hundreds of stars streaked from the heavens. The earth buckled as earthquakes, tsunamis, and volcanic eruptions destroyed Awakened and dark servants alike.

"Honi!" Arthur screamed. Fifty Shadule surrounded the old man. The Awakened no longer held the base of the mountain. The line had broken, and everyone was scattered. Honi screamed and dropped to his knees as the Shadule overwhelmed him.

"No!" Arthur shouted. Andreal charged through the fray, but groupings of spiny trees intercepted him. Within seconds the giant was gone.

Parker ran toward the trees, screaming in rage, but before he could get there, the ground split open, and he disappeared into a deep crevasse. Sage shrieked just behind Arthur. He spun to see her swatting at a swarm of flying and crawling insects that buzzed around Aliyah. Arthur sent a wave of light to clear the insects away as Sage and her sister dropped to the ground, covered in swelling bites. Sage struggled to her knees, trying to revive her sister.

"Get down!" Wild shouted. Arthur ducked as a flaming arrow passed just over his head. Wild tried to run to them, but a tornado smashed into him, hurling him away.

Arthur used the little strength he had left to form a shield around the five of them who remained. Sage, Aliyah, Arthur, and his parents were the last remaining Awakened in the valley. Dark servants attacked from every side.

His father dropped to his knees beside him as his mother wrapped her arms around all of them.

"I have never been so proud," his father whispered.

"Oh no," his mother said.

They turned to look.

A wave half as high as the mountain swept the valley, destroying every living thing. "It's over," Arthur said, hugging Sage close. The wave buried the dark servants and crashed into Arthur's shield. He only held it a few seconds before the shield buckled inward. The last thought Arthur had before he died was one of regret for not being strong enough to help his best friend.

"I don't understand." Tears stung Jack's eyes. "You're destroying it all. Not just the Awakened but your followers and the land—all of it!"

The demon's eye never left the destruction. "Did you truly think I cared about fame or riches?" the demon hissed. "I am a god, and those you call my followers are less than ants. This world is nothing. In destroying you humans, I have ripped out the Author's heart. If I cannot kill him, I will crush everything he loves." The demon turned its eye on Jack and Alexia, studying them a moment. "Yet maybe I was mistaken. If he truly loved you, he would never have allowed you to die at my hands."

Jack gasped as a tentacle pierced his chest.

"I am done with you," the demon crooned. "The war is over." Jack's eyes landed on Alexia; a tentacle protruded from her stomach. Her eyes glazed over even as she looked at him. "This mountain will be my throne, and I will spend eternity gazing upon my handiwork." The demon dropped Jack and Alexia to the ground.

Jack groaned as his eyes focused on his sister's body. The demon hunched over Jack and took the poet's pen, then slumped over to Alexia, where it retrieved the coffer.

While he lay dying, Jack realized his mistake. For the first time since this had all begun, he understood that he'd always had the wrong of it. Jack had fought the demon on its terms. He'd accepted Belial as the monster he claimed to be. The Assassin told the world he was all-powerful. He told the world it wasn't strong enough to stand against him, and the world had believed him. Though Jack had fought the Assassin before, he'd always accepted that he was the rabbit and Belial was the lion. And so they'd played out these roles as expected.

The world crumbled in a blaze of fire. Jack peered from the edge of the cliff. The oceans overflowed their banks, and he understood he was too late. The end of all things had come.

"It is finished!" the demon roared at the heavens. "The Children of Prophecy are dying, and this world belongs to me! Do you hear

me? I have won!" Jack's and Alexia's stars had faded and were no
longer visible above the slithering sky.

It's over. Alexia had fought as hard as she could, but the Assassin had
been too powerful. *There's nothing more we could have done.* She felt
death approaching. But Alexia Dreager held on. She willed herself to
stay alive just a few more seconds. She'd never been one to give up,
even when all was lost. The world had been destroyed. There were no
more Awakened and no more Shadow Souled. There was nothing but
fire and darkness. If Jack wasn't dead already, he would be any second.

The Assassin had deceived his followers into thinking they would
be kings and queens in his dark new world, but it had all been lies.
His only desire had been to hurt the Author.

Alexia couldn't feel her body. She was eyes floating in a decaying
world. The demon no longer stood over her, though she couldn't
move her eyes to see if it was still nearby. *"The Assassin only has the
power you give him."* The thought was dim. Alexia barely noticed
it. Death cradled her in its arms. She could feel its kiss. *"THE
ASSASSIN ONLY HAS THE POWER YOU GIVE HIM."*

Alexia blinked. She'd forgotten she knew how to blink. *So what?*
It was a tired thought. *Even if that's true, it's too late now.* Again the
thought pounded through her heart: *"THE ASSASSIN ONLY HAS
THE POWER YOU GIVE HIM!"* She'd heard it said many times by
Elion and Mrs. Dumphry. But she was dying. What did it matter
now? All she needed was to let go, and it would finally be over.

"No." Her lips didn't move, and her voice came out in the whisper of a whisper. Yet the word hung in the air. It had no more force than that of a butterfly's wings, yet inside Alexia it resounded with the strength of a hurricane. She blinked again as death loosened its grip.

"No!" she said more strongly this time. "I don't ..."—she stopped in exhaustion—"I don't give you the authority to kill me." A ripple ran through the pool of blood surrounding Alexia. Her chest heaved a deep breath as a trickle of blood flowed back into her body.

Jack would have gasped, but he had no strength. As his sister stood, the wounds in her body mended themselves, leaving only scars. There was a radiance about her that hadn't been there before. *She looks just like Mother.*

Alexia stumbled over and knelt beside him, grabbing his hands. She was speaking to him, yelling, but he couldn't make out the words. The end had come, and Jack was far too tired to fight on. He didn't know how she still lived, but it was too late for him.

The last thought Jack Staples had before he died was one of love. Love for his sister, Alexia. Love for his best friend, Arthur Greaves. Love for all who'd died in the fight against the shadow—his father and mother, Parker, Mrs. Dumphry, Elion, Aias, Wild, Andreal, and all the people he'd met along the way. With his last breath, Jack Staples was grateful.

Alexia pounded on Jack's chest. "He doesn't have the power! You just have to see it. Just believe! The Assassin doesn't have any power over us! Jack, please! You can't leave me," she cried. For a very long time, Alexia wept into her brother's chest. But Jack Staples was dead.

Alexia stood and looked around. The sky was slithering darkness, and the world was bathed in explosions of fire. There were no oceans, just fields of bubbling lava and black stone. Alexia Dreager was the last human on earth. She'd been too late to save anyone.

She clenched her fists. The Awakened might have lost the Last Battle, but she would not stop fighting. She would find the Assassin and put an end to him once and for all. She turned her gaze to the mountaintop. There was only one place he could have gone.

Alexia Dreager began to climb.

There is a space between life and death, a brief moment when the soul is detaching itself from the body. It is the space of a single breath where the body is not quite dead but is not really alive, either. And though it is only a breath, it can feel like a lifetime. Jack Staples looked down upon his body to see his sister collapsed atop him, weeping.

"I think that was my new favorite part!" A child's voice giggled in his ear.

The world flashed a brilliant white, and Jack was suddenly sitting on the greenest grass he'd ever imagined. Time sat Indian-style in front of him, giggling and looking at the sky. She wore a frilly dress, and her emerald eyes sparkled. Jack looked up to see a vision in the sky. Alexia Dreager wept over her brother's body as the world burned.

"What are you talking about?" he said. "The world is gone, and everyone's dead."

"Oh yes, that was terrible, all the fighting and whatnot. But I'm not talking about that part, silly. I'm talking about what just happened with Alexia! I don't think I've ever seen anything so beautiful."

"What's so beautiful about it?"

Time giggled again. "Alexia just realized who she is for the very first time. Not even Mrs. Dumphry or Aias, not even Elion fully understood who you humans truly are. Not since the poet himself has anyone fully embraced their true identity."

Jack shook his head. He had no idea what Time was talking about. "So I am dead. And it's all over, then. We lost?"

"Oh no! You haven't lost, silly! Didn't you hear what I just said about Alexia? He can't possibly hurt her now. And you can't be dead, or you wouldn't be here with me." Time snickered. "But, yes, your soul is leaving. Soon you will awaken in Siyyon, where you will begin a wonderful new adventure."

"But what does it matter if Alexia manages to kill the Assassin? The world is gone. The Awakened, the Clear Eyes, all of them!"

"What does the poet's blood do when it touches something?" A small smile curved the edges of Time's lips.

"But we lost it. The Assassin swatted it away, and it's lost. It's too late, don't you see? Mrs. Dumphry spent three thousand years searching for it for nothing!"

"What does it do, Jack?"

"It transforms whatever it touches," Jack said irritably. "The poet's blood gives life."

"And didn't he tell you his blood runs in your veins?" Time leaned forward, watching Jack with a mischievous smile.

"Yes, but what does that have to do with—"

Time's eyes widened. "Now you see it too," she said. Her smiled deepened as she looked up at the sky. Jack looked up to see his body lying on the black stone. Alexia was no longer there. The world flashed around him, and when he opened his eyes, Jack Staples was back on top of the mountain, and the vial of the poet's blood was lying beside him.

Alexia Dreager's star blazed in the dark sky. Besides the fires far below, it was the only source of light. The demon Belial lurked at the top of the mountain with its eye glued to the star just above. "Why do you still burn?" the demon sniveled. "She is dead! I don't understand. Why do you still burn?"

Jack's star exploded into life, its light bursting across the darkness. The light from the two stars grew even brighter until they blazed like the noonday sun. "No!" the demon gurgled. "It is not possible!"

From her hiding place, Alexia smiled. *Jack is alive. And if he is, he also understands the truth of it.* She stepped boldly from the shadows. "Belial," she said. She didn't shout, and she wasn't shaking.

The demon lurched around. When it saw her, it puffed out its chest and shrieked. At one time it would have caused terror to rise in Alexia, but as she saw it with true eyes, she was amazed at how puny the demon was.

"I don't know how you are still here, but this time I will make sure you are dead!" Belial lurched forward with beaks and spiked feelers outstretched.

Alexia almost felt pity as she watched the feeble thing. It truly believed it was a god. But now Alexia understood who she was. The Author's blood was in her veins. She stretched out her arm, and the demon stopped in midair.

"Impossible!" it gurgled, squirming like a squid. "You don't have the power to stop me."

Alexia walked slowly around the hovering demon, examining it. "It was all a facade." She shook her head at the absurdity of it. "You never had any power at all. But we believed what you told us."

"I won," the creature whined. "They are all dead. Even if you kill me, I have ripped out the Author's heart."

"Not true," a voice said.

Alexia smiled. Her little brother had come. When she turned to look at Jack, she almost gasped. Light radiated from him, and as he stepped forward, the demon whimpered.

"You almost won," Jack said, "but the power to destroy is nothing compared with the power to create." Jack walked over and reached inside the demon's ragged cloak, retrieving the Poet's Coffer. "I finally figured out what you trapped in here."

The demon's eyes grew wide. "No," it bleated, "you must not!"

Jack placed one hand on the top of the coffer and one hand on the bottom and then twisted. A small hole appeared in the top. "I was in the throne room five thousand years ago when you killed the poet. I watched you slam your fist into his chest just before he died. I didn't realize what you were doing until now." Belial wept as Jack reached back into his cloak and pulled out the feathered pen. Alexia watched in wonder as he placed the pen in the hole. "You understood that a single breath of the Author holds more power than you ever dreamed. So you used the coffer to capture the poet's final breath." A trapdoor in the side of the coffer slid open.

Alexia's heart sang as a small breath of wind left the coffer. The breath of the poet grew into a light breeze as it swirled around them. The blubbering demon snarled and hissed. "It burns! Please, it burns!"

"Is this really him?" Jack asked. "This is the thing we've all been so afraid of?"

Alexia nodded. She couldn't understand how they hadn't seen it before. The breath of the Author grew to the strength of a hurricane. Alexia was sure the wind would blow them off the mountain, yet she felt safely rooted to the ground. The demon howled and shrank in on itself, trying to escape the otherworldly gale.

Jack stepped up to the creature and looked it in its weeping eye. "This new world will be one of joy, laughter, dancing, and love. There will be no fear or death. And you are not welcome here." He reached into his cloak and produced the vial of the poet's blood. He smiled at his sister and then threw it high into the air. Lightning struck the vial, and the blood of the poet entered the storm. Blue, crystalline light filled the air as the storm grew ever stronger.

The demon snapped at the furious wind. "No!" Its beaks frothed and its tentacles squirmed. The crystalline wind whipped at its cloak. "No! It burns!" the demon screeched as it began to disintegrate. "It burns!" The final shriek came out in a keening whisper before the demon faded into nothing. For a long moment, Alexia and Jack stood in the midst of the gale, not saying a word.

"Not even Mrs. Dumphry realized what it means to be one of my children," a voice said. Alexia and Jack turned to see the Author standing in the midst of the hurricane. Radiance shone from him, and his eyes shifted through a rainbow of colors as they gathered the light. "My blood runs in your veins, and this war was won the very moment you embraced the fullness of who you are."

The Author walked to the children and knelt between them, placing an arm around each of their shoulders. *He feels like home,* Alexia thought as she leaned into him. The storm grew ever larger, but though she stood on the edge of a great precipice, she felt no fear of being blown from the mountain.

"May I ask you something?" Jack said to the Author.

"You want to know why I chose to show up now, when the war is over. You want to know why I let the world crumble."

"It's just that I don't understand," Jack said. "There was so much pain, so much loss, when you could have stopped the Assassin ages ago. You could have ended the war in the blink of an eye. He never had any power at all."

The Author's eyes gathered even more light as he smiled. "I could have, but there's nothing more beautiful than watching your children become who they're meant to be. I was by your side every moment of this battle. I lent you my strength when yours failed. I whispered encouragement to your hearts, and my hand guided your steps. But if I had fought this battle for you, you'd never have learned the truth. This life, this world was merely a beginning. And though the Assassin caused great pain, you and your sister have found a faith that's unshakable, and that's more beautiful than anything in all of creation."

Alexia wasn't sure what was about to happen, but her heart sang as the poet looked into her eyes.

"Are you ready?" he asked.

"Ready," she said.

The Author looked to Jack. "And you … Are you ready?"

Jack nodded.

"Then join me in creating this new world. Let your breath join with mine." He motioned to the raging wind. "Breathe into the storm."

Both children exhaled a long breath. Their breath mingled with the Poet's Storm as the Author extended his arms and the gale blasted down the mountain. It was the beginning of all things. It was the breath of creation. Where the wind passed, the world sprang into life. The breath flowed into the destroyed valley as bones began mending themselves and torn flesh was stitched together. Lush grass exploded from the ground as mighty trees formed in a matter of seconds. The Poet's Storm howled through the valley, bringing life where it passed.

Waters receded to reform their banks as the oceans teemed with new life. The Poet's Storm continued to blow across the earth as the dead rose again and the Assassin's Shadow dissipated. The sun shone bright on this new world, yet it wasn't the only source of light. Each blade of grass, every tree and stone, every last bit of earth radiated with the light of new life.

The wind was a force like the world had never known as the Poet's Storm swept across every land until the earth had been transformed.

Arthur Greaves was rather enjoying death. In many ways, it was far more exciting than life. He regretted that the world had been lost and the Assassin had won, but there was nothing to be done about it now. And this new world was far more fantastical than anything he could possibly have imagined.

"We could spend a thousand lifetimes just discovering how this world works!" Sage said. She looked different. She was as beautiful as ever but was also more radiant and carefree.

Arthur stood with his mother and father and Sage and Aliyah. He'd already seen Andreal and Wild—and everyone else, for that matter, except Jack or Alexia. He'd been searching for them, but they were nowhere to be found.

Something pulled at Arthur. He turned to see what it was, but nothing was there. Then it happened again. Something was pulling him back. "No," he yelled. "I don't want to go! I want to stay here!" But he couldn't keep his feet rooted, and he burst away in a streak of light.

When he opened his eyes, he was back on earth; he was sure of it. But it had changed. In many ways it had become like the world he'd just left.

"It's incredible," a voice whispered from behind him.

It was Sage, looking as radiant as ever. "Oh good! I'm so glad you came back too. I just couldn't bear to be here without you."

Sage gave Arthur a kiss on the cheek. "I like you very much, Arthur Greaves."

"So what do you think?"

Arthur spun to see Jack standing with a grin parting his lips. Mr. and Mrs. Staples stood beside him, and Alexia and her parents were there too.

"Jack!" Arthur nearly jumped with joy. "It's so good to see you!"

"It's good to see you, too." Jack laughed.

"I don't understand," Arthur said. "What happened? How did you finally defeat him?"

"By realizing he was far too pathetic to fight in the first place," Jack said. "Now what do you say we go home?" He placed a hand on Arthur's back. "I want to add another board or two to our tree fort."

"Do you mind if we join you?"

Arthur turned to see a man striding up the valley. His eyes shone like the sun, and Elion and Mrs. Dumphry and Aias were at his side. "It's the Author," Arthur said.

Mrs. Dumphry was no longer an old woman but was young and beautiful with fire-red hair.

"It will be a long walk back to Ballylesson," the Author said. "But that should give us plenty of time to catch up. Arthur Greaves, do you mind if we join you and your companions on the journey home?"

Arthur sputtered for a long moment as Jack and Alexia started to laugh. "Yes!" Arthur almost shouted. "Yes, please!" Soon all of them were laughing, the Author most of all. Arthur looked at Sage and Jack and all of his friends. "I don't know," he said, "but I think this might be the perfect ending to the grandest adventure I could have imagined."

The Author nodded as he placed a hand on Arthur's shoulder. "Arthur Greaves, this is only the beginning. The best adventure is yet to come."

Imagine a far more fantastical world than the one you know—a world that boils just beneath the surface of your ordinary life, if only you have the eyes to see it. This world is filled with giants, time travel, terrifying beast, and mythical creatures that have been at war since before time. Now, imagine you awake to this reality and learn you are at the center of it all; you are destined to both save the world and destroy it. These are the stories of Jack Staples and Alexia Dreager.